Ten Short Stories

by Nine Authors

Edward Grosek

Ten Short Stories

AuthorHouse™
1663 Liberty Drive
Bloomington, IN 47403
www.authorhouse.com
Phone: 1 (800) 839-8640

Ten Short Stories: by Nine Authors, edited by Edward Grosek

Published by AuthorHouse 4/20/2016

ISBN: 978-1-5246-0329-8 (sc)
978-1-5246-0436-3 (e)

Library of Congress Control Number: 2016906126

Print information available on the last page.

This book is printed on acid-free paper.

authorHOUSE®

Ten Short Stories

by Nine Authors

edited by Edward Grosek

Foreword

My motive for compiling and publishing *Ten Short Stories* was to provide a conveyance for authors of short fiction that runs longer than 1,300 words, the upper limit for submissions to *The Rockford Review*.

I contacted several writers I was acquainted with and offered to each a place in the book. For an encouragement –an inducement –I extended to each the opportunity of including an illustration to go with his or her story's text.

Here was a proposition one should not refuse, yet some of the writers declined!

Turning down an (almost) guaranteed acceptance to publish makes no sense. Anyone with aspirations to be a creative writer should immediately recognize the value and expeditiousness of an invitation from an editor to get into print. For spending time shopping among the literary magazines and reviews for suitable publication vehicles and then submitting to one after the other is wearisome and frustrating –and expensive.

Anyone avid to show off and promote her or his artistry should, instead of refusing an offer or procrastinating over it, get to work –in our case with pen and paper.

The various characters of the stories in this anthology experience conflict, risk, competition, and self-discovery. We think Guy De Maupassant would have enjoyed owning and reading this book.

Edward Grosek
egrosek@stny.rr.com

Contents

My Winter in Britain, with Caesar

by Paul Smith

I wanted to be tough in high school. I was, in a way, but not like some of the other guys. Once I saw a junior push in front of Metzger in the cafeteria line. We were sophomores. Metzger put his finger through the guy's belt loop in back and hoisted it up about six inches. The junior yelped like a girl. The rest of us laughed. Then Metzger pushed him back where he came from. People like you when you're tough. I've never seen Metzger in a fight, but everybody respects him. Even the priests here at Loyola like him. I was going to say they respect him, but the Jesuits don't respect any of us sophomores, not even if you are first string on the football team that won the lousy Red Division this fall and vice-president of Sodality like Metzger is. Being tough was natural for him. Not for me, though.

One day we had a fire drill. It was the middle of January. We had just gotten our books out of our lockers, gotten a glimpse of father Beall patrolling the halls for latecomers, and arrived at Father Dunn's Latin class. Metzger was with a couple other jocks in the front of the room. They were laughing about something. They got quiet as I got near. I hate that. Schoeneker came in just as I sat down and opened my Latin book to Chapter Eleven of Caesar's Gallic wars. Schoeneker was my height, but slimmer and less of a jock than me. I went out for cross country. He didn't seem to care if anyone liked him, and the funny thing was they did. I watched Metzger to see if he would shut up with his jock friends Scala and Fieberg or keep talking. As Schoeneker went past, Metzger hauled off and slugged him on the shoulder to show him he liked him even if Schoeneker wasn't tough like the jocks. I put my nose back in the Gallic Wars.

Class hadn't started yet, and Father Dunn hadn't arrived. Suddenly Metzger left Fieberg and Scala and came over to talk to me. "Nice sweater, Smith," he said. I couldn't tell whether he was joking or not because Metzger always smiled. It was like he was playing a joke on the whole world. "Is that wool or the new polyester crap?"

I knew it was wool, but I wasn't going to let him know I knew. That wasn't tough. Anybody who was a jock knew that. Even I knew, and I wasn't a jock. You weren't supposed to know if the sweater your mother bought you was wool or polyester or even rayon. You just put the thing on when it was cold and forgot it. Or better yet, you *didn't* put it on when it was cold so that the guys could see you were so tough you didn't need one. But then I saw Scala and Fieberg with sweaters on so I decided having one was alright.

"It's just a sweater," I told him.

"Nice looking," he said. He touched the sleeve and started rubbing the material between his fingers. Scala and Fieberg laughed to themselves. I pulled my arm away.

"What's the matter, Smith?" he asked me as the smile went from his face. "Did I hurt you?"

"Hell, no."

"You're awfully touchy, aren't you? Maybe I should just forget it. Yeah, let's forget the whole thing."

He started to go back to Scala and Fieberg. "What? Forget what?" I asked.

He stopped. I couldn't see his face, but I could see Scala and Fieberg. Their faces lit up as a look got passed between them. Metzger turned around and came back.

"I was really admiring your sweater. You know, you've got a good build. Almost as good as mine. I was thinking, 'Hey, that sweater might fit me if I asked Smith to borrow it, just to try it on to see if his build is as good as mine.' But then I thought, 'Nah, he won't let me.' Then Speedy Scala told me, 'Hey, he does have a good build, so go ahead and ask him.' So what do you say? Could I try on your sweater?"

"What? Are you cold?" I asked. I wasn't going to make it easy.

"I just want to try it on. But as a matter of fact, it is cold where I sit. Very definitely. Cold." His smile came back.

"You sit in the middle of the room. In front," I said. "Right here it's cold," I nodded to the window beside me.

"Yeah, but you have a heater here, too, along the floor. Up front, for some strange reason, we have a breeze, and it's cold. Brr, is it cold. If I could borrow your sweater, just for Latin class, I'd appreciate it." He punched me on the shoulder like he hit Schoeneker. "Good build, man."

Metzger's reasoning sounded pretty funny to me, but if jocks like Scala and Fieberg needed sweaters, I guess he did, too. I took off the sweater and gave it to him. My shoulders were getting a lot bigger. I worked out after school.

"Wool," Metzger said as he looked inside the collar. "That's the best kind, Smith." He threw it over his shoulders. I started comparing how he looked in the sweater compared to me, but gave up. He was a jock. He smiled and went back to his desk just as the bell rang and Father Dunn came in.

The jocks didn't like Father Dunn. He was not like the other priests at Loyola. It was his first year here, and he wasn't used to things here. That's what I heard. How would I know? This was my second year, and I really didn't know anything about anything. Loyola was only for guys. It was supposed to be special because it was all Catholic and up in rich Wilmette, which is safely outside of Chicago. I wasn't that crazy about it, but I liked Father Dunn.

Father Dunn was that age between young and really old, a big span, somewhere in the middle. He wore glasses, had a sarcastic smile, and a way of putting you down so that he was the only one who enjoyed it. One day we had a surprise Latin test. We all did terrible, and Father Dunn picked out one bad test paper and read it aloud to us. "'And Caesar crossed the Rubicon on a forced march with three legions of soldiers, archers and galley slaves.' Now, one might ask oneself what galley slaves were doing three hundred miles from a galley, which you would normally find on a ship. Unless one is so tired or pre-occupied with football practice that the sense of the translation doesn't mean a damn thing to him." Then Father Dunn crumpled the test paper up into a little ball and dropped it into the wastebasket. The room became dead quiet, and he told us the test wouldn't count. Normally, that would have caused a riot of applause, but the room stayed quiet, and everyone felt uneasy because he said 'damn'.

I liked him, though. He didn't play up to the jocks like Father Bowman and Father Boyle did. He put the jocks down and didn't try to get a laugh out of it like the other priests. The priests all had their own lunchroom, but one day I saw Father Dunn eating lunch in our cafeteria. He sat at a table all by himself.

Father Dunn came in, went up to his desk where he made the sign of the cross and told us to stand up.

"Oh, Lord, we thank Thee for this day that we might partake in Thy knowledge and we ask Thy blessing that our wisdom might serve You better. Amen. Be seated."

Father Dunn looked briefly at the ceiling, left the desk and walked directly to the center of the room. He was tall and lean, lonely and gaunt in his black cassock before us. I experienced a sudden, terrible fear that this was the kind of lonely man I would become when I got older and discovered that I had no friends. I was glad I'd given my sweater to Metzger.

"Does anyone have any idea what Caesar's frame of mind was when he spent his first winter in Britain?" he asked us. "He describes the cold for us in Chapter Eleven, and his best friend Maximus has just been killed. Yet he still has hope, doesn't he? Is he brave, or just pretending? Is he being brave for the other soldiers? Would anyone care to comment?" He scanned the room with his narrow nose pointing from one side to the other, unable to find a hand in the air.

It was the kind of question we could b.s. our way through, but nobody liked to answer the first question in class. It was like you were a brown-nose if you did.

Finally, Metzger's hand went up in the front of the class. His arm looked really good in my sweater, especially at the shoulder. His muscles were well developed, like he'd lifted a lot of weights. But then, so were mine. I did pushups after school. They were tougher than weights. I dropped cross country because it made me throw up. But I still did pushups.

Just as Father Dunn was getting ready to call on Metzger, the fire alarm went off. It was funny. Fieberg looked at Metzger almost as if it wasn't a surprise. I was behind them, but I could see each guy lift his head up slightly the way they said hello in the halls when Father Beall was around and you couldn't say a word. Father Dunn looked at the clock and the door and said, "Stay calm, everyone. This is just a routine fire drill. We'll file out the door and into the yard by the door beside the gym."

Everyone got up. I was going to freeze to death without my sweater. "Metzger," I half-said, half-whispered.

"And no talking."

"Can we get our coats?" Sennet said.

"No coats and no talking."

Father Dunn led us out of the room into a busy but rather quiet hall. Sometimes the halls were noisy because the lockers made lots of noise, but not now. All the classes were being taken out into the snow. There were black cassocks all over the place, shoving guys into lines and shushing us. It was like a prison movie. Father Beall cruised up and down the hall, supervising us and the black-cassocked priests and looking for somebody to say just one word. No one did. Everyone was thinking to himself it was twenty degrees out and sometimes the fire drills took an hour.

As soon as I followed Schoeneker out into the yard, I felt the cold air go right through my thin shirt. Metzger was ahead of me. Father Dunn got us all in line in the yard as it filled up with shivering students.

"It's a bomb," I heard Scala whisper to Schoeneker. "Somebody put a bomb in the basement."

'No talking," Father Dunn said as he passed us. "Mister Scala, I'm watching you."

I had to find out what was going on. Scala shut up. The only one between me and him was Schoeneker. Everything we did was in alphabetical order. I knew more about the back of Schoeneker's head than his own mother. Scala, Schoeneker, Sommers, Sennett. I knew when they all got haircuts. But I couldn't say anything while Father Dunn was right here. The L-shaped courtyard formed by the gym and the east wing was half-full, and there was nothing but us and the silent cold. Father Beall disappeared into the east wing again, but Father Dunn stood there shivering with us in his frayed black cassock. I had to be careful. One thing about the Jesuits – they popped out of nowhere when you didn't expect it and heard what you said. I did not underestimate them. We didn't move for ten minutes.

Then we heard the siren from a fire engine or a police car on the street beside the campus. I was going crazy wondering about what was happening. Scala said a bomb. Why were we standing here right where it could explode? Every time the wind gusted, the cold went deeper inside me. My hands were in my pockets, my ears were ready to fall off, and the wind went right through my shirt. The worst thing was that Metzger probably knew, and he had on my sweater.

Finally Father Dunn went all the way to the front of our line, by Adams and Barton. I thought I saw Adams turn around to say something. As soon as Father Dunn went beside Adams I asked Schoeneker, "What bomb? Where?"

"Shut up."

"Come on, I'm freezing my ass off. What bomb?"

Without moving a muscle he whispered back at me. "We're going to get the rest of the day off. It's a false alarm."

"Who did it?"

"A guy from New Trier."

"New Trier!" I didn't have any friends up in Wilmette or Winnetka. But maybe the guys from St. Joe or Faith Hope did. "New Trier," I repeated, as it started to make sense.

Then I felt a big hand on my shoulder. "You are the one I want," a deep voice said. I didn't need to turn around to recognize that voice, but I did anyway and saw Father Beall standing above me, with that wise Jesuit smile of his. The grip on my shoulder tightened.

Nobody said another word for five minutes until Father Bowman came out to whisper something to Father Beall that not even I heard, and my shoulder was still in his cold hand. Then Father Bowman and Father Dunn started marching everyone back into the east wing.

Everyone but me.

Father Beall stayed right there above me in the cold yard and waited till it was just me and him and the wind.

"Do you have any idea," he asked, "of the danger and the disruption you have caused today? And the expense, and the embarrassment?" With each inconvenience he poked a stubby index finger into my chest.

"I didn't do anything."

"New Trier, you said. I heard you say it twice. Somebody called in a bomb scare so everyone would get the day off. It didn't work. We just had the campus checked, and there is no bomb. And we're going to stay here until you tell me which of your friends at New Trier did it, and who at Loyola knew about it."

"I don't have friends at New Trier. I live in Skokie."

"That doesn't make any difference," he scoffed. "You can have friends anywhere. You're young."

"I didn't do a thing."

"Both knowledge and action bear the burden of guilt. And we're staying here till you tell me." One look at him, tall, stern, built like a linebacker, told me he could last longer than I could in this cold before giving in. I wished I'd never asked Schoeneker a thing. I looked at the windows in the east wing, expecting to see faces, but there weren't any. Everyone was back in class.

Father Beall didn't budge. Something had to get me through this. Toughness wasn't it. I thought of Caesar in Britain. How tough was he? He was tough. Whatever Caesar did there had to be nobler than standing out in a schoolyard getting disciplined. I could be like him, noble, proud, a Roman. What did Father Dunn say? Caesar was being strong for himself or for the other soldiers, and he was sad because his friend died. That's what I was doing, being strong for me and my friends. I was protecting them, whoever they were. Protecting who? Nobody. I hated them, hated Metzger, hated Scala, hated Fieberg. They never included me in anything. The only reason I was being tough out here was so the guys in class would say I was tough. Now I was really miserable. Caesar was tough, and I was just plain stupid. As the wind blew through me for the umpteenth time I decided that being tough for others was when you liked them and didn't care what they said afterwards.

We shivered together another half hour, until I heard a bell ring outside and knew it was eight fifty and time for classes to change. A minute after that the door beside the gym opened, and Father Dunn came out. I was numb as a block of ice.

"Can I have a minute with Mister Smith?" Father Dunn asked.

"Go right ahead," Father Beall said. I think he was glad he could go inside. But he didn't move.

"How about if we go inside, father," Father Dunn asked.

"We're good here."

"I don't think it was him. Smith isn't that kind of guy."

"He knows something. New Trier. He said 'New Trier.'"

"He's from St. Lambert's in Skokie."

"Everyone has friends at New Trier. They're right next door."

"Heck, I don't," Father Dunn smiled. "I'm new here. I don't have any true friends here yet. I think Smith's a good guy, but not too many people know it yet. And I don't think he has a friend at New Trier who'd do anything this stupid. Smith's smart."

"If he's smart, he can tell us who's in league with him," Father Beall replied.

"Sure, but why not inside? I'm freezing."

"When Augustine went into exile in Africa he spoke of the 'purity of isolation' and how it shaped his beliefs. He says so in his 'Confessions'. Maybe the purity out here in the yard will help Mr. Smith confess."

"Let me take him inside to my office. I see him every day. With your responsibilities here, you don't see him as often."

"He needs to come clean."

"Yes, of course. I don't approach things as directly as you do, Father, but at St. Mary's, we were strict as well." He put a firm hand on my shoulder. "You know what I mean?"

Father Beall's face softened. "Of course there's another way." The priests looked at each other. What do priests think about, anyway? "That way works, too," Father Beall said. "Let me have just one word with you."

Father Dunn and Father Beall walked a few steps away and had a few private words together. Now I really had to be tough. They were getting ready to pull the old

Inquisition routine on me. Now there were faces in the windows above, unsmiling faces behind semi-opaque glass that half hid them and their sentiments. The windows were frosty. The fluorescent lights inside made them glow. Then Father Beall went in and left me and Father Dunn shivering in the yard.

Father Dunn motioned to me with his head, and I quickly followed him back into the east wing. We went past the gym and its trophy case outside full of trophies, past the chapel, past the reception desk, and then someplace I'd never seen before, the priests' living quarters through a door on the far side of the chapel. Trophy case – full of awards, plaques, little statues that looked like Ignatius of Loyola but were football players. The trophy case had a big void in the middle, like it was ready to receive another trophy. We climbed a stairway to the second floor, passed a statue of someone, probably old St. Ignatius of Loyola himself, down another hall to a plain wooden door that led to a tiny room that had block walls painted light blue like our classrooms, a bed, a dresser, a desk and a crucifix on the wall. He hadn't taken me to his office because he probably didn't have one.

He pulled the chair away from his desk and pushed it toward me. Then he went out and came back with another one for him to sit on. I sat down and started rubbing my arms for the blood to start going through them again.

"Cold out there isn't it?" he smiled. "I came here from St. Mary's, in Atlanta. The warm weather spoiled me. It's hard for me to get used to this climate."

For a second I thought he was going to say it was hard for him to get used to Loyola, but I didn't say anything. I just sat there.

"Didn't I see you wearing a sweater in the hall before class? A red sweater?"

I couldn't remember if I'd seen him or not. I knew that all I had was a second to answer, and if I took longer than that he knew I would be lying, so I said, "Yeah, but I hung it up in my locker. I only needed it on the bus. Those buses are cold."

He nodded intelligently and said, "I saw a sweater just like it on Metzger. That's a coincidence, isn't it?"

"Really?" my voice rose. "I didn't notice."

"Now who do you think had that bomb scare called in?" he asked.

"Beats me," I shook my head.

"Maybe someone who's popular, with lots of friends here, and at New Trier maybe, friends who could make a phone call because New Trier starts class a half hour after we do, at eight thirty?"

"Look, I can explain about that New Trier thing. Schoeneker told me he should have gone to New Trier and not here. Stupid things like this don't happen there, he said. I'm not knocking Loyola or anything. It's just what he said."

"I don't care if you knock Loyola," he said. "I'm not that crazy about it myself. Schoeneker's from St. Alphonsus in Chicago, by the way, so he couldn't possibly go to New Trier. They've talked to Schoeneker, and he said it was Metzger. I'd like you to confirm it. It's not a sign of weakness to tell us. It's not snitching or anything. It's actually a sign of being smart."

Suddenly, I didn't like him. He was lying. I don't think they could have gotten to Schoeneker that fast and I didn't want anyone to think I told on Metzger, especially Metzger. I'd never have any friends.

"I don't think you really like Metzger," Father Dunn told me. "But you think he's a neat guy because he's on the football team that won the Red Division and he has a lot of friends. You'd like him to be your friend, wouldn't you? That's why you lent him your sweater."

"No," I said. "It's in my locker."

"We can always check," Father Dunn told me. "But I don't want you to think I don't trust you. I could use a friend or two myself." Father squinted at me from behind his glasses, and from the lonely look in his narrow face I couldn't tell if he was talking about us being friends, or lying again, or talking about nailing Metzger because he didn't like jocks, or even him being the nice cop versus the bad cop with Father Beall in a cross-examining scene like I'd seen on television.

"I'd like to be friends, Father," I said. "But I don't know anything. You can ask Schoeneker."

Father Dunn's face became confused. "I told Father Beall I'd have some luck with you. Just give me a clue. If it was Metzger, just nod, blink anything."

I didn't move a muscle.

"Why would you protect somebody who takes your sweater and then lets you stand outside in the cold for forty-five minutes? Do you think a person like that is a friend?"

"It's not a matter of friendship. It's a matter of toughness."

"Yeah, I thought so. Caesar was a tough guy. He told us how alone he felt in Britain."

"He suffered for his friends," I said miserably, "Because they were really his friends, like Maximus. I don't have any real friends to lose. Not Metzger, not Schoeneker."

"There's me," he said. His face became intent.

"And I don't know anything, either."

"Here's what I'm going to do," he said, adjusting his glasses and fixing me with a stare. 'We're going to call Metzger in here and tell him you confessed. Let's see if he stands up for you the way you stood up for him."

"No!" I shouted. "He won't." But the thought I had was that he would admit having done it, and then everyone would have thought I squealed. Metzger would get expelled, and I would be more alone than ever. Everyone would think I'm not tough. Metzger wasn't my friend, and never would be, but I had to look strong. I couldn't get out of it.

"I know he won't." Father Dunn said.

"So do I," I said. "Because I did it!" I looked him right in the eye. "I had a friend at New Trier call in the bomb scare."

"I don't believe you." His face was blank.

My stomach felt empty like the yard between the east wing and the gym. "It's the truth."

"You're lying to protect someone who doesn't even like you."

"You lied to me about Schoeneker!"

"That was a different kind of lie." I watched his thin lips form the outline of a sad, sarcastic smile. "That was a Jesuit lie, a lie that was meant to help you." He stopped smiling. "You'll get expelled for this."

"I don't care."

His face kept that same expressionless stare, the look of somebody who was puzzled and as alone as I was. "Alright, Eddie, I swear I'm trying to help you, but if this is the way you want it, this is the way you'll get it."

"This is the way I want it." I could barely hear myself.

He shook his head once. "Let's go."

We went back out, down the stairs, past the reception desk, the chapel, left to the north wing to Father Beall's office. We passed another statue, this time St. Francis Xavier, another big saint for the Jebbies, who was probably martyred for being tough and strong in the face of a heathen and lawless world. I knew what was coming. I was getting canned. I'd transfer to Niles East High School. My parents would be sad. Maybe at Niles they'd erect a statue of me: 'Saint Eddie of Skokie. He stood up to the Jesuits.'

"Wait a minute here, Mr. Smith," Father Dunn told me as he excused himself going past Father Beall's secretary and into his office. After a few minutes, he called me in. I entered Father Beall's office and faced them. Father Beall looked solemn, and Father Dunn's face told me nothing. I think I let him down.

"Eddie," Father Beall said, "Don't do this. You're too good."

"No, I'm not." I looked around. The office was a lot like Father Dunn's room – the same blue paint, cheap furniture and this terrible holy attitude, like my whole life was a mortal sin.

"We're not going to report you to the police, even though they want to know who did it. We handle our own problems our own way. One last time, Eddie. Help us?"

"No."

"Then you must leave Loyola. You realize that?"

"Yes," I said. My voice was like a wisp of smoke, vanishing out of my throat into the frozen cold of this school I'd hated ever since I got here. If this is how it had to end, then it could end right here.

"Then you are officially expelled," Father Beall said. He got up and crossed to the other side of the desk. "Come with me."

The nine-fifty bell rang at precisely the moment he dragged me out of his office and down the hall to where I figured he would throw me out the front door. Father Dunn hurried behind us.

But he didn't. He pulled me past the other sophomores, juniors, seniors, and even the lousy freshmen all rushing around between classes. He took me directly to my locker.

"Clean it out," he said. Then he spun around and waited defiantly behind me, his hands on his hips in his black cassock, waiting, hoping for some student to laugh, smile, or even just move his face wrong. One of the things I'd miss at Loyola was the sound of guys getting thrown into the lockers before class in the morning by Father Beall when he caught them talking. It was almost musical.

I fumbled with the lock a minute. The combination numbers spun in my head. Then Father Beall reached under his belt and pulled out an enormous key ring, moved me aside, and unlocked my locker. I reached for the books.

"That's exactly what I told you!" Father Dunn told Father Beall. "He's covering up. There's no sweater there."

Just then Metzger turned the corner our way from the east wing. Voila! With my sweater.

Metzger took one look at me and at them and said, "I didn't do anything."

"You are wearing Smith's sweater," Father Beall said. His voice resonated with about five centuries of righteousness, moral superiority, bombast and bluster. Right now, it sounded good.

"So what?" Metzger said. "He said I could have it." Metzger took off the sweater and coolly handed it back to me. He was as calm and collected as Father Beall. I had to give him credit.

"I didn't say anything because I didn't know anything," I told Metzger.

"Shut up!" His face turned and became a snarl of anger. "Just shut your goddamn mouth!"

"I did!" I shouted back.

"I told you it'd work," Father Beall told Father Dunn as he grabbed Metzger by the ear and pulled him down the hall out of sight. Father Dunn gave me a sad look and said, "I'm disappointed, Eddie, but I understand." He quietly closed my locker and put his arm around me. "I'm disappointed I had to lie to you about Schoeneker. Things like this are bad for everyone. Get to class."

I put on my sweater and hurried up to English class on the second floor. Everyone was at the window, watching something outside, even old father Skiffington, who was so old the only things that interested him were the *New York Times* book reviews and the debate team. I went beside Schoeneker to see what it was. Outside, shivering in the yard between the east wing and the gym were Metzger and Father Beall, eyeball to eyeball in a state of frozen silence. Here was a chance to see how tough Metzger was compared to me. I had lasted nearly an hour.

Metzger gave in in a minute and a half. He just shrugged his head like a broken convict. I was dumbfounded and completely baffled how to feel. I couldn't feel good no matter what Metzger did. But I still couldn't believe anybody as tough as him would give in.

"I don't believe it," I told Schoeneker.

"He doesn't care what anyone thinks of him," Schoeneker said.

"Yeah, he does," I said quietly. "He wanted to be known as the guy who got away with calling in a bomb scare and getting us off a day of school."

"You're both chumps. We watched you out there. Nobody fools the Jesuits."

Right before class ended, there was a knock on the door. It was Father Bowman. He talked to Father Ryan, our English teacher. Then Schoeneker and two more guys in our class got up and walked out.

An hour later I saw them plus Scala and Fieberg cleaning out their lockers, plus Metzger.

"Hey, I'm sorry," I said, coming up from behind. "But I didn't say anything."

They all looked at me like I was a germ. "You got caught," Metzger told me. "Remember that story about the Greek soldier with the fox? He let the fox eat his guts before squealing? That should have been you. That's all it took. But if you want me to forgive you, I guess I'm a big enough man to do that." He made a mock sign of the cross and then reached behind my neck to sort of flip the label inside my sweater. "You and your wool sweater are forgiven."

I was furious. I forgot who I was and who he was and put my face up to his and said, "You can go to hell." I was shaking I was so mad.

His face changed like I hadn't seen it do before. It was like he was unsure what to do and then had to cover it up by putting on the grand act. He slammed his locker door shut and left with the others. I expected him to say something smart or sarcastic, but he didn't. He just turned the corner and disappeared. And I thought that was that.

But it wasn't. They were gone for a week, but then came back, were reassigned to different home rooms, and life went on. I didn't figure it out and was afraid to ask anyone. But one day I passed that trophy case and saw the Red Division trophy for first place in football and figured that had something to do with it. Metzger and his friends were sophomores and juniors. If they came back next year....

For a month I kept raising my hand in Latin class, because I really thought I knew why Caesar felt so lousy in Britain during his first winter. But Father Dunn didn't call on me even when I was the only guy with his hand up. I think we both knew something. It was like a secret between us, and it was the only thing we shared in the coldest, longest winter I ever knew.

The End

Paul Smith lives near Chicago with his wife Flavia. He has had his fiction and poetry published in *Packingtown Review, Oyez, The Rockford Review, Ink, Sweat & Tears* and other magazines. He likes riding the bus and the subway in Chicago.

Miss Lonelyheart Pays Back

by Michael Humfrey

When I was divorced by my wife and banished from what they always call the "marital home", I moved into a flat on my own. This had the advantage of cutting in half my daily journey to work; but it also signaled for all the world to see the loss of everything else I valued in my life. I did not want to be divorced: I did not want my wife to marry another man: and I did not want to lose the comfortable home I had shared with her –happily as I had thought –for nineteen years. It took several plain-spoken meetings with my solicitor before I was finally persuaded that my marriage was over.

My flat was one of five created by the subdivision of a dark Victorian house which sat four square at the bottom of a cul-de-sac on the outskirts of the town in which I worked. My neighbors were a varied lot: there were Hazel and Dennis, both retired inner-city social workers, whose view of human nature reflected the sheer hellishness they had been exposed to every day of their working lives; Edith Eves, a prim, desiccated little woman in her late fifties, whom I occasionally passed scuttling from the local bus stop to the refuge of her front room; Charles Windrush, a solicitor who, like me, had been ejected from his own house by a heartless wife bent on marrying another man;

and my blonde and rouged landlady who lived alone on the ground floor in the largest of the flats and retained the garden for her own use.

I believe that most men, at the end of a bitter and protracted divorce, welcome the prospect of living alone for a time while they construct a new life for themselves. Charlie Windrush was one of them. He met his most urgent physical needs twice a month by paying a visit to a London "sauna" which he knew: otherwise, he preferred to be on his own. I was not like that at all. I am what used to be called "the marrying kind". I like the state of matrimony. I wanted to marry again.

It did not take me long to discover that this was easier said than done. The ways men and women meet each other when they're twenty-one do not apply when you're forty-six. It is not a matter of the goalposts having been shifted by the years; the truth is that it's an entirely different game.

Fortunately, I did not need to be told that the nightclubs of my youth –in fact the places where I first met my wife when we were students –did not cater for single, middle-aged men. I spared myself the embarrassment of learning this at first hand. But my attempts to meet single ladies in more acceptable ways were no more successful. I joined the local amateur dramatic society and was allowed to help paint the scenery; I attended meetings of Greenpeace and the RSBP; I went on a three-day guided tour of English cathedrals; I volunteered to help Friends of the Earth clear a nearby village pond of the detritus of ages. But after a month or two of this I was left feeling that, in the whole wide world, I was the one living person who lacked a partner and who was actively seeking one. Everyone else seemed content with life as they found it. I was the odd man out.

Then one bleak Saturday night, when it all seemed more hopeless than ever, I remembered the lonelyhearts page of the local Sunday newspaper –a page which, in the old days, I sometimes scanned on idle Sunday mornings after breakfast with a sense of amused detachment. I recalled occasionally reading out to Carol some especially crass and pathetic advertisement which made me laugh. Now, I waited impatiently for Sunday morning to arrive.

At first light, I walked out to the newsagent on the corner and bought a copy of the paper.

The Introductions page was divided into two columns: Gentlemen seeking Ladies, and Ladies seeking Gentlemen. It was clear at once that there were more of the first than the second, but I was not discouraged. Then, halfway down the Ladies seeking Gentlemen column I found this:

Very attractive 40 year old blue-eyed blonde, character actress, small private income, divorced, no children. Enjoys travel, reading, cooking, walking, good wine and conversation. WLTM a professional man of similar interests aged 40-50 …

It took me a minute or two to decipher WLTM. The text was followed by a box number. I delayed my breakfast, made another cup of coffee and wrote off at once, describing myself and my present circumstances at some length and asking for a photograph in return.

The reply arrived three days later. The photograph enclosed was a holiday snap of a pretty blonde woman looking back over her shoulder on a river bank and laughing at the photographer. She was wearing white shorts, sandals, a sea-green blouse and sunglasses. The note thanked me for my own letter –and hoped that I would phone her at the number she enclosed. Her name was Yolanda. "I think I know just how you must be feeling after your divorce," she wrote. "I've been there myself, and I've learnt that it is one of those things one really has to experience personally to understand. I hope I will be able to help soothe the hurt in some degree. Please phone me any evening at 8.00 p.m."

I think it was a measure of the state I was in that –when it came down to it– it took some time to screw up my courage to the point where I felt I could dial the number and hold an adequate conversation with the person at the other end. Already my imagination had come into play. I began to picture our first meeting, an evening at the theatre, walking in the autumn mist …

The voice was warm and welcoming when I phoned at eight o'clock that evening. She had just come in from a walk in the park. She had been looking forward to my call. She was sorry she hadn't got a better photograph to send me: it had been taken last summer on a visit to her sister … After a while, my anxiety seemed to fall away:

I suddenly felt at ease. I told her about my work, that the new town council chamber had largely been designed by me, that I found life on my own difficult to adjust to …

We spoke for about twenty minutes on that first occasion; then she said she had to go. She would phone me tomorrow at the same time. She said she had enjoyed talking to me, and she was sure that there was lots more to discover about each other. She was going to be in the centre of town next morning and she would visit the new council chamber to inspect my work …

From then on, we spoke to each other every evening, taking it in turns to telephone. She had indeed gone to the trouble of visiting the council chamber. She had liked the new colour scheme and the pale oak benches I had introduced. "You must be very proud of it," she said. I remembered that Carol had not even bothered to look at the drawings when I brought them home one evening before the work began.

It was clear to me from our first conversation, I think, that I had found a soul mate. She understood exactly my feelings about the break-up of my marriage and the pain of being rejected by someone I loved and trusted. By the end of the week, I found myself confiding in her thoughts I would never have shared with anyone else I knew.

She never directly asked me any question: it was the warmth of her voice and her concern, more than anything else, which served to draw out of me all the hurt and resentment which had festered inside since my divorce. "Yes," she would say, "yes, I understand exactly. It has all been so unfair to you. You did everything you could possible do. You were betrayed by someone you trusted: no one deserves that. I am just glad that I am here to help you in any way I can …"

Naturally, I wanted to meet her at once. But in this, as in everything, she was wise and discreet. "I think we should really get to know each other first," she said softly. "Let's make sure before we take that step. In the meantime, we can speak every evening –and I am beginning to feel that I know you well already."

I was importunate: I wanted to set a date. It was suddenly more important to me than anything else in my life. She laughed when I told her this. "All right," she said. "Let's both agree if all goes well we'll meet in two months time."

I took out my diary and named a date.

"Yes," she said. "If all goes well."

I would never have believed it was possible to fall in love with someone over the telephone –not at the age of forty-six. Get to like them a lot, yes; to admire them, perhaps; to look forward all day to talking with them in the evening, of course. But to fall in love with them? I would not have believed it.

Over the weeks that followed, our conversations became more intimate. I found myself telling her secrets of my adolescence and my parents' broken marriage that I had never revealed even to Carol in the early days of our own marriage, when I swore that there was nothing I would not tell her about myself and my thoughts. Now I wanted Yolanda to know every detail of my hopes and dreams –and my disappointments. No one else knew, for instance, that I had been deeply hurt by having to share credit for the design of the new council chamber when I could have managed the job entirely on my own.

The day we had agreed to meet came closer. We spoke about where we should have dinner. She preferred that we should meet at a restaurant: she would find her own way there. Perhaps I could take her home later on. I booked the table.

I was fifteen minutes early. It was a busy Friday night. I sat watching the door of the restaurant. People came and went: around me, the place filled up with diners. A family party celebrating someone's birthday took their seats at a large table behind me. I waited for more than an hour before I could bring myself to admit that she was not going to turn up.

There was a telephone in the passage that led down to the toilets. I called her number: it was engaged and it took me more than fifteen minutes before I finally got through to her.

The voice was unrecognizable. I found myself speaking to a different person: ice cold, uncaring, dismissive.

"I decided to call it off," she said. There was no apology, no hint of regret. I begged for an explanation. What had I done to offend her?

"I don't have to give you an explanation," she said flatly. "In fact, I don't have to give anyone anything." Then she put the phone down. When I rang back a moment later, her number was engaged. People squeezed past me in the passage on their way to the toilets. From the dining room, I could hear shouts of laughter from the birthday guests. I tried her number again: it was still engaged, as I knew it would be. I realized with a terrible, sickening certainty that my affair with Yolanda had run its course.

In its own way, this rejection was as painful as my divorce. The divorce, at least, had not been entirely unexpected: there had been warning signs, even if I had chosen to ignore them. This new calamity arrived without notice. I had built up in my imagination the elements of a new life, even a new marriage. I had pictured the new friends we might make, where we might go on holiday together, even the kind of house we might buy.

For a while, I nearly gave way to my sense of loss. Then Christmas came and I was carted off for a week by my brother and sister-in-law. They looked after me and let me talk it through, all at my own pace. When they returned me to my flat at the beginning of the new year, I began for the first time to seek new friends in a more conventional way. On Thursday nights I went to the local pub with Charlie Windrush. I joined the darts team. Then I got to know Hazel and Dennis in the flat below me. All three of us were competent cooks and we invited each other in for meals once or twice a week. After that, I never again felt the same bleak sense of despair which had threatened to overwhelm me. One evening, Hazel introduced me to her sister, who was herself divorced, and we started to see each other regularly. Neither of us spoke of marriage, but we shared a number of interests and were comfortable in each other's company. I had never had a lot to do with children in the past, but I seemed to get on well with Beryl's boys and, on Sundays, we often went out together very much as a family.

About two months after what I came to think of as the "Yolanda episode", our postman mixed up a delivery of letters to the five flats. Amongst my own mail, there was what I took to be my usual quarterly telephone bill. I was on the point of making out the necessary cheque when I realized from the size of the total figure that it could not be mine. The invoice was for more than three hundred pounds. Then I saw that it was intended for Edith Eves in the flat across the hall. I was about to return it to its envelope and slip it into her letterbox, when I noticed something familiar about the subscriber's phone number. I looked more closely. It was a seven-digit number permanently engraved on my memory. It was Yolanda's number.

Attached to the bill was the usual statement of itemized calls: it ran to five pages. Reluctantly, I spread the sheets out on my desk. Listed there, on every other evening for a period of eight weeks, was my own number. And then I saw that mine was only one of six or seven other regular numbers, all local and all contacted on alternate evenings at the same fixed times between 6 and 10 p.m.

I sat there at my desk with the bill in my hand, my face flushed scarlet, hoping without hope that a simple explanation might still occur to me. But slowly, inexorably the penny dropped. I understood it all.

After a while, I got up from my desk and crossed to the window which overlooked my landlady's garden and the front steps of the building. A bus drew up at the top of the road and a few minutes later the sad, stooped figure of Edith Eves emerged from the gloom of the unlit cul-de-sac and scuttled up the steps. Across the hall I heard the door of her flat swing open and then close behind her. Strangely enough, the only coherent thought in my mind was: I wonder where she found the photograph she sends to us.

The following evening I had been invited to have dinner with Hazel and Dennis. I brought with me two bottles of wine and waited patiently until we had finished the meal –and the wine. In the glow of their log fire, fortified by coffee and cognac, I deliberately steered the conversation towards the peccadilloes of awkward neighbors.

I recounted an anecdote about the people I had lived next to when I was a student. I was glad, I said, that I now lived among normal people. Dennis took the bait.

He hauled himself upright in his chair. "Normal?" he said incredulously. "You think our neighbors are normal? Then you haven't met Edith Eves."

I admitted that this was true.

"That is a lady with a problem," he said. "She hates you and me –I mean she hates all men. She once told Hazel that a man had destroyed her life ... and the inference was clear enough."

"What did the man do?" I asked.

Dennis poured us another brandy. "The usual thing," he said. "Promised her the earth, made her pregnant, fixed the wedding date –then phoned up while she was getting into her dress to say that he had changed his mind. He wouldn't tell her why. She never saw him again, never had an explanation. She still doesn't know ..."

Hazel came in from the kitchen with a fresh jug of coffee. She had been listening to our conversation. "It wrecked her self-confidence," she said. "She'd been a promising young actress: after that, she found she couldn't face an audience again. She had a late abortion: they botched the job. The man ruined her life. She's the unhappiest person I've ever known ..."

I got back to my flat at midnight. I walked over to my desk and extracted the telephone bill from the drawer in which I had locked it while I decided just how I would use it to confront Miss Edith Eves. I had thought I might simply knock on her door in the morning with the bill spread open in my hands. Now, I folded it once on my desk, tore it in half and then in half again. I dropped the pieces in my rubbish bin. The telephone company would send her another one in a week or two.

Of course I felt sorry for all the other unwitting men on her list, all doomed in turn like me to suffer the bitter shaft of her revenge –the only pleasure that remained in her ruined life. But in the broad scheme of things, rightly or wrongly I thought, wasn't it just possible that her need might be greater than theirs?

The End

Michael Humfrey's novels have been published in England by John Murray and in the United States by The Overlook Press. His short stories have appeared in *The London Magazine* and in literary magazines in the United States, Canada, Australia, and New Zealand. He is an authority on Caribbean marine mollusks and the author of *Sea Shells of the West Indies* and of *Portrait of a Sea Urchin*.

Family Confessions

by Joy Rewold Schneider

Running from my car across the frosted driveway and up the back steps, I burst into the kitchen still managing to balance a plate of pastries.

"Hi, Mom! Boy does it ever smell good in here!" I said, as I placed the confections on the kitchen table.

"Thank goodness, you are here. I've been worried about you driving from Notre Dame on Thanksgiving Day," Mom said, giving me a quick hug and then returning to embrace her stove.

"Yeah, the roads were a little slippery," I said, as I stripped off my coat and hung it on the back door.

"Well, thank God you made it here safely. Now, go wash your hands and help me get the turkey dinner on the table. Everyone has been hounding me to eat," Mom said.

Then turning towards the family room, Mom shouted over the televised football game, "Michele is home. We can eat now."

Back from the TV room came all kinds of responses with Tony, my younger brother, being the loudest. "It's about time!"

As everyone headed into the dining room, I was welcomed with the usual family greetings. Dad, looking like he was heading to work in his starched shirt and knotted tie, planted a kiss on my forehead as he passed me on his way to the head of the table. Antoinette gave me a big sister hug, and then helped me get the last steaming hot dishes on the table. Tony threw me a high five when I set the mashed potatoes next to the turkey in front of him.

"So glad you finally made it. I was afraid we were going to have to wait for Santa to come before we could eat," Tony said, never taking his eyes off the bronzed-skinned turkey.

"Very funny, Tony. Being a big senior in high school, I thought you would have outgrown him by now," I said, as I messed up his straight black hair.

The room was full of mouthwatering aromas from the various juices pooling in serving bowls, until Nana appeared, releasing her over-perfumed fragrance.

"So where should I sit?" Nana deafeningly questioned, as she was slowly entering the room with her walker.

"Sit between Michele and me, Mom," my mother screamed back, as she placed her apron on the back of her chair and smoothed out her dress.

"Which one?" Nana wailed, looking between Antoinette and me.

"Here Nana next to me," I said, pulling out her chair. "By the way Antoinette, I like your short haircut."

"What?" Nana interrupted loudly and then continued, "I'm sorry but I can't hear anything even with the darn hearing aids."

Turning back to Nana, I responded in a powerful voice, "You are sitting here next to me." Helping Nana into her seat, I was the last to be seated.

The dining room table wore our usual Thanksgiving dress: white linen tablecloth, turkey facade china, and cut-crystal goblets.

"Let's hold hands, while your dad says grace," Mom said, smiling at him from the opposite end of the table.

With that, Tony leaned into Dad as he took his hand and pleaded, "Dad, remember to keep it short. We don't want the food to get frost bite."

Dad glared over his bifocals back at Tony and then bowed his head. He began, "Dear God. Today we give thanks for your many blessings: Michele's safe journey home from law school, Antoinette's new condo, Tony's acceptance to Notre Dame, Maria's cooking skills, and Nana's good health. May you please continue to watch over us as well as all your other children. And finally, bless us, O Lord, for this food we are about to receive, through Christ, our Lord. Amen." Suddenly the chain of hands was broken, and everyone made the sign of the cross before raising their bowed heads.

Tony snatched a leg off the turkey platter before he passed it to Dad and immediately took a bite.

"Boy, Mom, this turkey is delicious," Tony croaked as turkey pieces overflowed from his mouth. "And Dad, about that Notre Dame acceptance, I deferred it. Steven, Peter and I are going to travel for a year."

"This is another one of your jokes, right Tony?" Dad said, holding the gravy boat in his hands which stopped the flow of food around the table.

"No, I want to see the world," Tony exclaimed.

Diverting his attention down the table to Maria, Dad asked: "Did you have any involvement in this harebrained decision?"

Mom, with raised eyebrows, shook her head no.

"So, you came up with this all on your own?" Dad asked Tony.

"Yup, along with the guys," Tony replied.

"And just how do you intend to afford this?" Dad yelled.

"Hey Tony, if you join the service, the government would pay. That's how Grandpa saw the world," Nana suggested.

"And Grandpa was lucky to make it back home alive, and that was before ISIL. Now the world is too dangerous with ISIS for boys to be traveling," Mom blurted out.

"ISIL and ISIS –are they the same people?" Nana asked, but was cut off by Tony.

"Everyone says we shouldn't act paranoid about potential ISIS attacks, and that we should continue to live our lives normally," Tony said.

"And normal for you is college. So, YOU are going to college next year even if it's a community college and that's FINAL!" Dad yelled. "Let me remind you, Tony, you won't be 18 for another year. You know what that means in the eyes of the law? Your ass is mine."

"But," Tony started, with Dad finishing: "There is NO but! End of conversation, so help you God." Tony's head dropped, and he briefly stared at his food before taking another bite of turkey.

Then came the question I was dreading. "So Michele, how's law school going?"

"I hate it. In fact, I dropped out. That's why I was late today. I was busy packing up my stuff." Now, the room went completely silent. Everyone except Nana stopped eating and looked at our little corner of the ring, waiting for Dad to explode.

"What's going on?" Nana asked, elbowing me. "I can't hear a word anyone is saying."

Patting her hand, I repeated in the best lawyer voice I could muster, "I quit law school. I want to be a pastry chef."

Nana squeezed my hand and said, "That's nice. I love pastries."

"What?" Dad barked so loud that even Nana jumped. "For clarification, you are blowing a full ride at Notre Dame to become a baker?" Then turning to Mom, he continued, "Did you know about this, Maria?"

"No, I'm just as surprised as you are," Mom responded. Then covering her eyes with her hands as she leaned on her elbows, she cried, "No one tells me anything anymore."

"Yeah, I know what you mean," Nana said, lightly touching Mom's bowed head. "Of course, I never really know if they didn't tell me, told me but I forgot, or told me but I didn't hear it correctly. It's so confusing," Nana said, with a sigh.

"Well, we sure as hell heard what Michele said so let's focus on that. So Michele, would you please state for the record what in the hell you are thinking," Dad asked.

"I've tried to like law for you, Dad, but I just can't do it anymore. Law school is bland, stale, and distasteful. Law is smothered with buttery terms to preserve the rich and dissolve the poor," I said, as I looked down at my half eaten turkey dinner.

"Is that really your testimony? No one likes law school," Dad laughed as he sat back in his chair.

"Maybe, but I don't like anything about law. I want to be creating gorgeous desserts that taste fabulous and give people pleasure. I don't want a life of charging people for wordy living wills, healthcare power of attorney forms, and other legal documents which they can get on the internet for free! And I certainly don't want to encourage scamming large sums of money from people through uncalled-for lawsuits."

"Let me call your attention to the FACT that you are only ONE semester away from graduating. You must proceed and at least FINISH," Dad shouted as he leaned forward. His hot breath circled my head.

Looking up at him, I shook my head no and said, "No, I have over a year because I've been catering this whole semester."

"You've been what?" Dad gasped.

"I'm sorry Dad, but law isn't my passion. It's yours. I don't want to spend any more time studying law and writing: 'hereintofore after referred to as...' And I certainly don't want to study for a bar exam which I will never need," I said.

"Anthony, can't Michele do other things with a law degree without taking the bar," Mom asked Dad, trying to reach a compromise.

"Of course, she could be a research assistant or a law librarian, but I certainly would never have sent her to college let alone law school for her to end up in the kitchen frosting cakes," he said.

"This is great, Michele. Now what am I going to do it I ever get arrested? I was counting on you to help me if I had any trouble on my world trek next year. I know Dad wouldn't even accept my phone call," Tony said, as he gave me a downcast look from across the table.

"That's damn right. So you had better never end up in jail," Dad roared, waving his index finger at Tony.

"Jail? Are you in some kind of trouble?" Nana asked me.

I patted Nana's hand again and said loudly, "Nothing that requires a lawyer. Do you want to try some of the pastries that I made?"

"Sure, I love sweets," Nana said with a big grin.

"Me too. Excuse me while I get the tray," I said, as I got up from the table.

"You sit down. I'm not done with you yet," Dad said, pointing his right index finger now at me.

"You can continue interrogating me over dessert," I said standing firm.

"I don't get it. I love law. In fact, I'm planning on running for judge. Do something, Maria. Michele is throwing away a great career! I know she is just doing this to get back at me for encouraging her to accept the law scholarship at Notre Dame," Dad said.

"Dear, even if you were a judge, you can't make her stay in law school," Mom said, as I walked out of the room.

"Well, I'm the JUDGE in this family. So do something!" He yelled loudly enough that I heard him in the kitchen.

"What can we do, Anthony?" Mom said, as I returned with my sweets.

"Yeah, what can we do? Arrest her?" Tony asked.

"Who's getting arrested?" Nana asked.

"Tony, if he doesn't keep his mouth shut," Dad sharply responded. Pounding his fist on the table like a gavel, Dad turned to Tony. "That's enough out of you, Mr. Wise-guy, or I'll hold you in contempt and withhold you allowance. And forget all this nonsense about traveling next year. You are going to college, like your sisters did."

Once the china finished its dance, I placed my tray on the table. "Here are some of the *patisseries* I have been selling on campus. I hope you like them," I said, passing the plate to Nana first.

"I love desserts," Nana said, snatching several.

"I object. You are just trying to sway everyone with your sweets," Dad said.

"Well, she sure gets my vote," Nana declared.

"Well, this is probably the best time for me to make my announcement," Antoinette said.

"Finally, the big sister has something to add to the conversation, and don't tell Michele she can move into your condo with you when I throw her out of the house," Dad said.

"I support Michele."

"Of course you would, you girls always stick together," Dad interrupted, waving his arms in our direction.

"Yes, as I hope you all will support me. I think everyone should follow their heart even if it takes one down an unlikely path," Antoinette continued.

"Well, I sure would say going from a lawyer to a baker is getting off the beaten track," Dad cut in.

"I'm not just talking about Michele. I'm referring to myself too. I have something to tell you all," Antoinette said, pausing to take a deep breath.

"Okay, proceed already. It can't be any worse then what we already have heard. One child is dropping out of college and another one doesn't even want to start," Dad said, pointing to me and then Tony.

Now everyone was looking at Antoinette waiting for her to speak, except for Nana who was eyeing all the pastries on her plate.

"I'm gay. I want to be called Andy from now on. And Sarah is not my roommate, she's my fiancée," Antoinette announced.

The dining room went dead silent except for Nana who shouted, "I love these cookies!"

"WHAT?" Dad asked, as his pupils became almost a large as his eyeglasses.

"These cookies are delicious. They remind me of something I've had before," Nana said, smacking her lips.

"Oh, I don't care about those damn cookies," Dad yelled.

"Oh, don't worry," Tony said as he padded Dad on the back. "This is just a phase. She is just experimenting with sex like a lot of my friends."

"WHAT! Don't tell me this applies to you too," Dad said.

"Oh no, I only like girls."

"Speaking of girls, my neighbors in the nursing home would love these cookies. Could you bring some of them over tomorrow?" Nana said, as she licked her fingers.

"Sure, how many?" I asked Nana.

"I don't know. Maria, how many residents are at Golden Gates? I want enough for all my friends and some for the staff."

"I think about 100 residents."

"Okay, Mom can you help me bake in the morning?" I asked.

"Don't get her involved," Dad said, wagging his finger at me. "And you," turning his finger toward Mother, "don't you encourage her."

"Why? Mom's great in the kitchen. You even thanked God for that gift earlier this evening," I responded.

"I object! I want to strike my prayer from the record, and you all need to disregard it."

"You can't withdraw a prayer," Mom said.

"Yeah, that's politically incorrect," Tony jumped in.

"Order, order," Dad yelled over everyone, pounding his fist on the table. "Let's get back to Antoinette."

"You mean Andy, don't you?" Tony corrected.

"Don't you say another word," Dad said as he grabbed Tony's arm.

"Hey, Andy, can you help me cater tomorrow at The Gates?" I asked.

"Stop this!" Dad said, as he rose up from his chair. "Don't get her involved in your foolishness. Didn't you just hear Antoinette, she has her own problems."

"I don't have any problems now that I don't have to hide Sarah any more," Andy said.

"How long has this been going on?" Mom asked Andy, as Dad sank into his chair.

"Sarah and I just celebrated our two year anniversary," Andy said.

"No, I mean this gay thing," Mom clarified.

"Since high school."

"See," Tony blurted out and then quickly shut up.

"I always wondered why you didn't want to go to your senior prom," Mom said, almost under her breath.

"Now what did you just say?" Nana asked Mom. "Even though I'm sitting right next to you, you know you have to speak up."

"Oh, never mind," Mom said, waving her hand.

"So, can Michele bring these delicious cookies over tomorrow or not?" Nana asked Mom.

"Who cares about those GOD damn cookies?" Dad yelled.

"You should, Anthony. I just remembered where I tasted them before. They are like your mother's cookies, only better," Nana shouted back.

"Yeah, Dad. I tweaked your mother's recipe. Try one." I said, as I passed the plate.

"Go ahead, Anthony, they won't kill you," Nana said.

"No, but my children are sure trying to!" Dad said.

"Oh, one cookie won't clog your heart," Nana said.

"Okay, just to put an end to this conversation so we can concentrate on Antoinette." Dad said, looking at Tony daring him to make a counter. Dad grabbed a cookie off the tray. Everyone stared as he took a bite. Dad chewed the cookie slowly while he examined the uneaten half in his hand.

"Isn't it wonderful," Nana said, taking another.

"You added chocolate chips," Dad said.

"Yup, I knew you loved these cookies and loved chocolate, so I combined them," I said.

"You know, I could help you package these cookies for grocery stores with my marketing degree," Andy said.

"Yeah, they wouldn't even have to be refrigerated since there aren't any eggs in them," I chimed in.

"Dad, you could help with the licensing and contracts," Andy said.

"Oh, yeah, I could make a variety — some with nuts, others with dried cherries and so on," I added.

"I could do the art work," Tony piped in. "This is an idea that we really could take to the bank," Tony said.

"Did you say Shark Tank?" Nana asked, and then went on: "I love that show. Sweetie, you should go on it with these cookies! But first Anthony needs to help you get a patent. The Sharks always want one at least pending."

"Wow, this could be a family affair," Mom said.

"What, is someone having an affair?" Nana asked.

"Oh, for Pete sake, I rest my case. Pass me another God damn cookie!" Dad shouted.

Grandma Shirley's Italian Cookies

Mix together: 1 cup soft butter (salted)
2 cups flour
1/2 cup powdered sugar
Add: 1 teaspoon vanilla
chocolate chips to taste (optional)
nuts to taste (optional)
dried cherries to taste (optional)
Make dough into small round balls and place them on an ungreased cookie sheet.
Bake at 350 degrees for about 20 minutes. (Don't over-bake them, they only need
   to be light brown.
When totally cooled, roll them in powdered sugar.
Serves about 2 dozen.

The End

Joy Rewold Schneider is a retired nurse. She received her M.S.N. from the
University of Miami, and has published several articles in professional nursing
journals. Currently, she and her husband live in Pompano Beach, Florida where
she continues to write for fun.

The Tree

by James Bellarosa

One hot humid morning an old man answered a knock at his door. A stranger in his mid-thirties was standing on his porch. He frowned and said to the old man, "I've come to take down the tree in your front yard."

"There *are* no trees in my yard."

The stranger raised his eyebrows, turned and pointed. "Then what do you call *that*?"

Puzzled, the old man glanced out at his yard –a lush green lawn that ran from the house to the curb. He turned to this strange man –his snarled hair and dirty trousers. "What do *you* call it?"

"That's a tentacle tree, and unless it's destroyed it'll seize your house!"

It struck the old man for a moment that this was a joke that someone was playing. But the evenness, the gravity of the younger man's voice, and his intense unsmiling expression were too sincere.

"I work for free," the latter went on, "so you'd be foolish to leave that menace standing. Besides, I need the work. It's what I do."

Nonplussed but curious now, and wary that this person probably mingled often with moonbeams, the old man, by nature a humane individual, sensitive to the frailties of others, conceded. He replied, "You know, I've tolerated that tree much too long. I'd be grateful if you'd remove it." He thought to himself, "Let's see what happens."

The stranger's lips thinned into a grin. "Thank you. I haven't worked for so long my self-esteem is trying to implode!"

"Where are... your tools?"

The stranger tapped his trouser pocket. "In my pocket," he said. "I'm eager to put them to work." He bounded down the porch steps and out onto the lawn.

The old man closed the door and went to his front window and watched as the stranger, looking upward, began walking in circles in the center of the grassy lawn, nodding his head, apparently assessing the "tree" and the job ahead of him. After a minute, he dug his hand into his pocket, withdrew it, and waved it from side to side over his head, as if he were cutting away branches of the tree. For several minutes the "trimming" continued, then the worker stopped and appeared to collect the fallen branches into a pile about ten feet away. Then, returning to work, he picked up his pace, swinging, then flailing his arm even more furiously in the air. The old man shook his head and wondered why it was that God would mix a man's marbles and then mock his malaise with mirages. He shrugged and went to perk some coffee.

Minutes later, as he was sipping his coffee, his next door neighbor –a good friend but a skeptical and sarcastic man –phoned and asked what was going on in front of his house.

"He's chopping down a tree he sees out there."

"What?!" There was a pause. The neighbor could not restrain himself. "But why is he chopping it down? It seems to be minding its own business."

"It's a tentacle tree, Earl," the old man answered. "It's got its eye on my house."

"Well, I have an abduction tree in my yard and it's got its eye on my wife," Earl scoffed. "If your Don Quixote comes anywhere near it, I'll slug him!"

He guffawed, and the old man ended the call. He returned to the front window and noticed that the worker had become even more animated in his efforts, bounding forward and chopping at the tree, then hopping back quickly, then repeating the same antic again and again, sparring with the thing. "Hummm," the old man sighed and sat down at the window with his newspaper.

In a while, the stranger came to the door sweating. He asked for some water.

"Have you run into a problem out there?" the old man asked, as he handed the man a glass.

"Nothing I can't handle," replied the stranger. "It's fighting back, trying to grab me, but you see, I'm too quick for it." He stood at the door, grinning. "Stay inside," he told the old man, "this fight is coming to a head and there'll be plenty of fallout when the showdown comes!"

It was another incomprehensible remark. The old man promised he would remain inside, and asked the stranger to finish up quickly. He cautioned him, "The sun and heat makes your kind of work risky."

The stranger finished with the water and returned to work; but as their brief exchange ended, the old man asked himself why he was going along with all this. He decided to call the local hospital and ask to speak with someone who worked with disoriented patients. When he explained the circumstances to the attendant who had answered the phone, he asked whether anyone was missing from the hospital's mental ward. The attendant laughed. "We had someone harmless like that once, but when he began moving mountains, we had to put him to sleep."

More sarcasm; the old man thrust the receiver down onto its cradle.

At that very moment, he heard calls for help from outside and looked out to see the tree cutter thrashing about as if he were trying to free himself from some invisible being. Bent forward at the waist, legs pumping, arms flailing, he remained stuck in place. Quickly the old man hurried out of the house and to the howling and struggling man.

"It's got me!" the man yelled, grimacing. "Help pull me free!"

"What's got you?" the old man asked.

"The tentacle tree! Pull me away from it! Hurry!"

Stupefied, incredulous, the old man began wondering about his own sanity –could he be dreaming? –as he reached for the stranger's arm and pulled.

"Pull harder! Hurry!" the panicked, desperate man shrieked.

Still unable to accept the lunacy of the whole situation, the old man almost turned away; but the stranger's resounding and unearthly pleas came charged with a terror he had never heard before. He tugged and yanked, but despite the frantic efforts of both men, the stranger was stuck somehow and would not budge.

"Go get help!" he pleaded. "Hurry up before it swallows me!"

Exhausted, the old man let go and ran next door.

He opened the front door and, without knocking as he usually did, entered and with fear in his voice now, called to his friend for help with the emergency in his yard.

"Calm down, Charlie," said his neighbor with a knowing smile, "and tell me again what that guy's doing. Pantomime?" Evidently, he had been watching through his own windows.

The old man blurted out, his voice trembling, "I'm afraid he's working up to a heart attack –on my front lawn! Come out and help!"

Earl sighed, rose deliberately from his chair, and followed the old man out onto his porch. "Where's your heart attack victim, Charlie?" he asked, grinning.

The old man looked at his property, across his yard from end to end. The stranger had vanished.

"I swear to God, Earl, he was over there and he couldn't move," the old man muttered. He gaped at his front yard, confused. Finally, he turned to his friend, whose tongue was pushing out his cheek and holding back his laugh. "You don't believe he was even there, do you?!" the old man snapped.

"Of course I believe he was there, Charlie," the neighbor drawled. "I can see the tree stump from here!" Earl belly-laughed. With long strides, he walked back into his house.

The old man turned and was about to follow his neighbor, then thought better of it. He turned again and went back to the spot where the stranger had so violently struggled. Looking down at the sod, he noticed that although it had been dug and chewed up, there was no trail or traction marks in the grass that would have been made by the dragging away of branches. As he looked about for any other sign of the man, a breeze picked up. A leaf drifted onto his shoulder. Not knowing what to make of all this, tired of it all, Charlie threw up his hands in resignation, but when he tried to head back to his house, he couldn't move.

The End

James Bellarosa has been a member of the Rockford Writers' Guild for many years and a prolific author even longer. He has received two Pushcart nominations, published three books of fiction, a novel, and two short story collections. Over the years in fact, he has published more than 175 short stories. Recently, Jim has been an active source of inspiration for other members of his writers' group.

Tye

by Bruce Muench

Our farm was located four miles south of the town of Marengo. Marengo is in northern Illinois and had a population in 1960 of 5,500 souls. The graveyard population was about the same. The main farm crops were becoming almost exclusively corn and soybeans, including the crops we grew, even though for the thirty-five previous years we had been a dairy farm. This is true of much of the Upper Midwest's agriculture domain.

The businesses in town at that time were mostly family-owned and very often handed down from one generation to the next. The main business district in town was centered in three blocks along State Street, just north of the railroad tracks. State Street is also Illinois State Route 23 and runs further north to Harvard, near the Illinois-Wisconsin state border.

Nearby Harvard is the main rival of the Marengo High School football team. It was also known at that time as the "Milk Capitol" of Illinois, because of its many dairy farms. However by 1970, the family dairy farm was becoming a thing of the past, along with one-room country schools and brick streets.

One of the seminal businesses in Marengo was the Coast to Coast Hardware Store, located in the middle block on the east side of State street. When I was twenty-five years old, the second floor above the Coast to Coast was occupied by the local telephone office. Within this office, with its thirteen foot high ceilings, was the main switchboard run by young women in their twenties and thirties, all busy plugging wires into switchboard holes while wearing earphones over their 1950's hairdos. If someone from out-of-town wished to make a long-distance call from Marengo, he was obliged to climb the steep staircase up to this room and to make his wishes known to one of the operators. That is neither here nor there to the thread of this story, because relatively few strangers would come to Marengo just to make a long-distance call.

More significant to this story is what went on in the store beneath the telephone office. The hardware store owner and manager was Carl Gustafson, a short, genial native son of Marengo. Carl was "manager" only by title, because the main driving force of the store was a woman named Tye Yerke. Tye was the principal clerk in the store and was the "go-to" person for anyone shopping for anything in that particular store. Any soul who lived in or around Marengo learned this fact of life quickly. In this period of time, when computers were just beginning to become recognized, middle-aged Tye already possessed a computer between her ears.

If a person came into the store bent on buying or renting one of the myriad store products, she or he soon came in contact with or was referred to Tye Yerke, simply because Tye knew where everything was –if it existed within the walls or in the basement of the building, whether it was a nail of a certain size or a paint of a certain color. She would also know the price of the certain article, or could conjure in her mind a reasonable price for it.

An encounter with Tye was somewhat akin to meeting Tugboat Annie, although Tye was not really a tough person, just a person short on words. I never heard her use profanity in all the years I knew her. A typical over-the-counter exchange with Tye went like this: a customer would enter the store and immediately come face to face with a woman of medium height wearing a loose-fitting, straight-draped cotton dress who would, without a smile or a "Howdy," say, "What?" He or she should have in advance a prepared answer to this inquiry, because there would be little or no additional conversation. If the customer could satisfy Tye with an answer, she turned on her heel and headed swiftly down one of the aisles. The customer then had to follow her just as swiftly and as long as he was able, because Tye *was being drawn inexorably* to the location of the desired object. A first-time customer might believe at this juncture that he is being abandoned in the dust by this brusque woman, but he is not. Tye *will find* and *will produce* the needed article, once her computer brain zeros in on its selected residence. But if Tye knew initially that the requested item was not within a city block of where she was standing, she would respond with, "We don't have it!" and proceed to the next customer, usually one showing, at that point, a bewildered look.

In conclusion:

Tye Yerke is representative of the kind of super-efficient clerks who in the middle of the twentieth century inhabited many of the small retail stores in America. She was a jewel that, I'm afraid, is not easy to find any more. She stored many gigabytes of memory in her brain and could do complicated mathematical equations therein, like Archimedes, sans adding machine. She represents individuality and entrepreneurship at its finest with her unique ability.

Tye was not the only store clerk of this quality in Marengo. There was Bobby, a short man of Italian descent, who owned the shoe repair shop just a block south of the Coast to Coast. Bobby's store space was piled high with customer shoes, his shop looking much like a hurricane had just exited; yet he would ultimately find the shoes you brought in just a month ago, if you would just be patient. Likewise there was Levin's Clothing a few doors north of Bobby's, in its second generation of family ownership. A few blocks north of the railroad tracks there was a man who repaired small engines in the shop behind his home. If you went into his establishment, you would find it necessary to navigate around an assortment of small engines in various stages of disassembly on his cement floor; however, he, like Bobby would eventually repair your engine and at a fair price... just be patient.

I think there's an underlying moral to this story and it bears on our present, "have to have it now!" frame of mind. First, it has to do with the dignity of serving others, and second, it has to do with having patience. Maybe these values are gained with age.

I have noticed in recent years that the most knowledgeable and most helpful clerks in stores seem to be the most elderly ones. They are the ones who will walk you, the customer, to the exact spot on the shelf where your requested item resides. They are also the ones most likely to carry on a conversation with you about the current weather and how it is affecting the condition of their cars, or their arthritis. I, for one, think that is nice, because I have arthritis too.

The End

Bruce Muench, retired now in Roscoe, Illinois, was a professional aquatic biologist and an amateur photographer. He writes, "I began writing and experimenting with prose and poetry at age seventy. Now, I'm beginning to realize that the term 'closure' is the same thing as 'ad infinitum'."

A Day in Dallas: "What if" - the Eternal Question from History

by Alan Youmans

November 22, 1963 dawned crisp and clear in the Dallas-Fort Worth, Texas area. President Kennedy had spent the night in Fort Worth. His schedule called for him to attend a breakfast there before departing on a short flight to Dallas later that morning. He and his wife Jackie, along with Texas Governor John Connally and his wife Nellie, would ride in the lead limousine of a motorcade parade through downtown Dallas. The motorcade would then proceed to the Dallas Trade Mart for a luncheon speech. After the speech the entire presidential entourage would board Air Force One for the return trip to Washington DC.

This reason for this trip was to gain political favor in Texas in preparation for the upcoming 1964 Presidential Election. Vice President Lyndon Johnson, a Texan, recommended President Kennedy make this trip. Texas was definitely a divided state in regards to Kennedy and the Democrats. Johnson, the master politician, knew the charismatic presidential couple would make a positive impact on the Texas populace. Fact be known, Jackie Kennedy was a bigger sensation than the President, a reality not lost to either Johnson or Kennedy's chief-of-staff Kenny O'Donnell. As Texas would be a key state in the upcoming election, Kennedy agreed to the trip.

§

J. D. Tippit was a 39 year old Texas native and an 11 year veteran of the Dallas Police Department. He had served in the 17th Airborne Division in World War II and was decorated with the Bronze Star. During his time on the police force he was cited twice for bravery. He and wife Marie had been happily married for 17 years with three children. Tippit's current patrol area was in the residential area of Oak Cliff south of downtown Dallas. This morning he was also on call as back-up for the downtown area, for many of the Dallas police force were assigned for crowd control along the planned presidential motorcade route through downtown Dallas. Large crowds were expected.

Jack Ruby was the proprietor of the Carousel Club nightclub located in downtown Dallas as well as the Vegas Club in the Oak Lawn district north of downtown. He was 52 years old and had been born in Chicago as Jacob Rubenstein. He had a troubled childhood with multiple juvenile delinquency and truancy episodes, spending sporadic time in foster homes. Jack was drafted into the army in World War II and served honorably as an aircraft mechanic. After the war he returned to Chicago before moving to Dallas in 1947 and changing his name to Jack Ruby. He went on to manage various nightclubs and strip clubs. In the course of his business dealings he had developed many ties to Dallas police officers who frequented his establishments. Ruby was single, never married, with no children.

Lee Harvey Oswald was, to say the least, a complex individual. Maybe confused would be a better description; definitely frustrated with his life. He was 24 years old, born in New Orleans. His father died two months before Lee was born. His mother Marguerite moved Lee and his older brother Robert multiple times among New Orleans, New York City and Dallas. Lee experienced a variety of problems growing up and for a short time was placed in a juvenile reformatory in New York for truancy. He was described as being withdrawn, temperamental and confrontational. By the age of 17, he had lived at 22 different places and attended 12 different schools. Lee quit school at 17 and joined the Marine Corps to be trained as a radar operator. He was eventually stationed in Japan where he taught himself Russian.

After receiving a hardship discharge allegedly based on his mother's care needs, Lee embarked on a series of bizarre actions. He defected to the Soviet Union in 1959. Though the Soviet authorities were initially suspicious, Lee managed to convince them to let him live there. He eventually was assigned to work as a lathe operator in an electronics factory in Minsk. Lee eventually married his Russian wife Marina in April 1961. Apparently disillusioned with Soviet life, Lee, Marina and their baby daughter successfully applied for immigration back to the United States in June of 1962. They returned to the Dallas area with little public notice, much to Lee's disappointment.

After multiple job failures in Dallas, Lee returned to New Orleans in April of 1963. Marina's new found friend Ruth Paine later drove a pregnant Marina and her daughter to New Orleans to join Lee. In late September 1963, after Lee experienced more failed jobs and a baffling association with the "Fair Play for Cuba" political front organization, Ruth Paine moved Marina and the baby back to Ruth's home in Irving, Texas. Lee then took a bus trip to Mexico City in an even more puzzling attempt to obtain a visa to go to Cuba. When the visa was refused, Lee returned to Dallas in October, 1963.

One of Ruth Paine's neighbor's, Wesley Frazier, worked at the Texas School Book Depository in downtown Dallas. Frazier helped Lee get a job there as an order-filler on October 16. Lee and Marina were experiencing marital problems. So during the work week, Lee stayed at a rooming house in Oak Cliff, south of downtown Dallas. On Friday nights he would ride with Frazier out to Irving to stay with Marina at Ruth Paine's house. Then on Monday mornings he would ride back to Dallas with Frazier.

On Wednesday afternoon, November 20th Roy Truly, the School Book Depository's building manager, approached Lee Oswald on the sixth floor as Lee was filling an order. "Hey Lee, how's it going? Did you know President Kennedy's motorcade is driving right by here on Elm Street this Friday?"

Lee looked up and replied, "Hi Roy. Really? Sounds like a big day for Dallas. We should be able to get a real close look as he passes by."

After exchanging a few more pleasantries, Roy left to check on other employees. He didn't see the wry smile forming on Lee's lips.

Jack Ruby looked around the Carousel Club. It was close to 11 pm of Thursday night, November 21st, and he was smiling his familiar wide grin. Business was really good, better than usual. Jack thought to himself, "Must be all the people in town to see the President's parade through Dallas tomorrow. Thank you Mr. President!"

Jack gave a quick call to his other establishment, the Vegas Club up in Oak Lawn. Business there was also exceptionally good. Even though it was only Thursday, he decided to drive up there around closing time. He didn't like the idea of leaving the unusually high nightly cash receipts on the premises before the weekend even started. One thing he had learned in Chicago was not to encourage robbery by leaving a lot of money on the premises. It was common local knowledge that Jack was armed when he was carrying money. Additionally, he had a good relationship with the Dallas police. It was also rumored Jack Ruby was somehow connected to the Chicago mob.

Besides, Jack always liked going to the Vegas Club; a slightly different clientele frequented that establishment. Even in 1963 Dallas, the Vegas Club had a good reputation within the homosexual community; though the word "gay" was beginning to gain favor as an acceptable term. Bottom line, Jack enjoyed their unconventional sense of humor. Plus, they liked to spend money.

It was well after 2 am when Jack left to drive up to the Vegas Club, north of downtown Dallas. He had placed the Carousel Club's plentiful nightly receipts in the Carousel's office safe. As the Carousel Club was located in the downtown area, close to the main police station, he felt the money was secure. Ruby told his bar manager he was going up to check on the Vegas Club. He instructed the bar manager to close up when the last customers left. Jack planned on coming back later to the Carousel with the Vegas Club receipts for deposit in the office safe. Depending on the time, he would either go home or sleep on the cot in the office. Jack wanted to watch the President's downtown parade scheduled for the following noon.

Jack arrived at the Vegas Club a little after 3 am. There was still a large crowd having a good time. Even though official closing time was 2 am, Jack had an "understanding" with the police. Besides with the presidential visit, even more slack was in effect. Many of the regular customers heartily greeted Jack on his arrival. Jack's club manager nodded to him; it had been a very lucrative night. Ruby smiled and nodded back. It looked like it was time to have a couple of drinks with the customers.

§

Friday morning November 22nd, Lee Oswald woke up before his wife Marina did. He had unexpectedly ridden back to Irving with Wesley Frazier the night before. Usually Oswald stayed at his boarding room in Oak Cliff during the week and came back to Irving on Friday night. The only explanation he gave Marina and Ruth Paine was that he missed Marina and the children.

Lee was very quiet so he would not wake either Marina or the new baby. Quietly he dressed. Before leaving, Lee took off his wedding ring and placed it in a small china cup on the top of the dresser. He also took $170 in cash from his wallet and left it beside the ring. Then he went to the Paine's garage and brought out a long package covered with brown wrapping paper. He walked to the street curb where Wesley Frazier was waiting in his car.

Lee opened the back door, placed the package on the back seat and closed the door. As he got into the car on the passenger's side he greeted Frazier, "Morning Wesley."

Wesley replied, "Good Morning Lee. What's in the package?"

Lee casually said, "Just some curtain rods for my room in Oak Cliff. Remember I told you that was the reason I came back last night. Let's get going. You were the one who wanted to leave early for work today."

Frazier nodded, "Oh yeah, I remember. Yeah with the President's parade today there will probably be more downtown traffic. You know how backed up it can get around there."

Lee sarcastically responded, "Sure, we don't want to delay those important text books from getting delivered on time."

§

Officer J.D. Tippit was also up earlier than usual. Tippit's shift sergeant had instructed all his men to be on patrol an hour earlier. With the upcoming presidential motorcade through downtown, heavier traffic and large crowds were expected along the planned parade route. As a designated back-up, J.D. was expected to handle normal police calls to free up the assigned patrol officers to maintain visibility along the motorcade route.

Therefore Officer Tippit was on duty by 6 am. He purposely located himself along the southern portion of the downtown area, a little north of his regular Oak Cliff patrol area. Even though the President was not scheduled to arrive at Love Field until 11 am, traffic was noticeably thicker and people were starting to arrive at prime viewing points along the announced parade route. J.D. wondered whether he would get lucky and see the President and Jackie drive by.

§

Jack Ruby shook his head again. He was trying to keep awake as he was driving back from the Vegas Club to the Carousel Club downtown. The late night customers at the Vegas Club did themselves proud partying. It took all of his and the club manager's persuasive skills to get the last of the revelers out of the Vegas Club around 5 am. Then it took another half hour to close up the club and reconcile the night's cash receipts. Jack also had to retrieve his dog sleeping in the office and carry her to the car along with the briefcase of cash receipts.

Jack was driving south from Oak Lawn on Turtle Creek and Cedar Spring Road. He was going to cut over to North Field Street and then over to Houston. Once on Houston he could proceed downtown and take a left onto Commerce to get to the Carousel Club. There he would deposit the cash receipts in the office safe. Ruby decided he would sleep on the office cot and get up to see the presidential motorcade as it passed by a block away on Main Street. Just before reaching the Continental Avenue intersection something caused his dog to suddenly wake up with a yelp. This caught Jack by surprise and almost by reflex he turned his sleepy gaze towards the dog, thus failing to recognize and respond to the red light at the intersection.

§

Since leaving the Paine house in Irving, Lee Oswald maintained his silence. In the short time Wesley Frazier had known Oswald, such behavior was not surprising. Wesley just accepted Oswald's moodiness; experience had shown Lee would talk when he felt like it.

Frazier had traveled along Irving Boulevard to North Riverside Boulevard and then onto Continental Avenue. Wesley smiled to himself. Traffic was becoming more dense as they approached the downtown area. Wesley didn't expect Lee to compliment him on the decision to leave early. As they approached the intersection with Houston Street, the light had already turned green. Wesley slowed to make the right turn onto Houston.

Suddenly without warning, Jack Ruby's car barreled through the intersection and struck the left rear part of Frazier's car; causing it to violently spin to the left, across the lane and into the opposing traffic lane. This exposed Oswald on the passenger's side to an oncoming delivery truck.

The delivery truck had no chance to brake or steer to avoid Frazier's spinning vehicle. It struck the car directly at the passenger's door, crushing Oswald on impact.

Officer Tippit responded to the emergency call and was the first to arrive at the crash scene. He immediately called for an ambulance, and additional police support. Even with his eleven years of experience as a police officer, J.D. was taken aback. This was a bad accident.

§

Officer Tippit pulled his police car in front of Frazier's smashed car; keeping the flashing red lights of his vehicle turned-on to warn the oncoming traffic. The delivery truck had stopped askew in the middle of the road beside Frazier's car. As the passenger side door was crushed inward, Tippit knew he could not open it. He approached the driver's door and slowly opened it. J.D. observed that Frazier was conscious, but appeared dazed.

In a clear, stern voice Tippit spoke, "Sir. Are you all right? Can you hear me?"

Frazier slowly turned his head towards Tippit, "I think so. What happened?"

Looking into Frazier's eyes J.D. responded, "Your car was hit by another vehicle. An ambulance is on the way."

Frazier slowly nodded his head.

Tippit then focused his attention past Frazier towards Oswald's unconscious body, "You in the passenger's seat, can you hear me?"

No response. Tippit could hear the sirens of the approaching police cars and ambulance.

Again speaking to Frazier, "Sir the ambulance is almost here. Hang on."

Tippit stood up and motioned the approaching ambulance towards Frazier's car. As the two supporting police cars arrived, J.D. motioned one of the cars towards Ruby's car now stopped on the other side of the intersection and the other towards the delivery truck.

Two ambulance attendants came up to Frazier's car and helped him out of it. As he could walk, one attendant helped him into the back of the ambulance. The other crawled in across the seat, lightly grabbed Oswald's left shoulder and shook him gently, "Sir, can you hear me! Sir, can you say anything!"

No response.

A minute later, the other ambulance attendant had returned. The two attendants managed to retrieve Oswald's still unconscious body from the wrecked car. With Tippit's help, the three of them placed Oswald on the wheeled gurney, pushed it over to the ambulance and loaded it into the rear of the ambulance. The ambulance then sped away with flashing red lights and blaring siren, on its way to Parkland Hospital.

By this time two more police cars and another ambulance had arrived on the scene.

Tippit observed that the driver of the delivery van was uninjured but understandingly shaken. The driver was standing by the van, talking to the police officer who had stopped there.

Tippit then looked across the street towards Ruby's car, noticing the front end was crumpled and the radiator steaming. Another policeman was talking to the driver, who was still in the car but apparently conscious and coherent. The second ambulance had stopped and the two attendants helped the driver out of the car and into the ambulance.

As the driver was emerging from the disabled car, Tippit recognized him as Jack Ruby. Even though Tippit had never met him, he knew Ruby by reputation. Tippit shook his head slowly. At this point two wrecker trucks arrived to retrieve the involved vehicles. Tippit turned his attention back to getting the accident scene cleared and getting traffic safely flowing again, remembering that this was the morning rush hour.

The two other recently arrived police officers had positioned themselves to direct traffic around the accident scene. One wrecker truck was preparing to remove Frazier's car; the other had stopped by Ruby's car. The policeman talking to the delivery truck driver yelled over to Tippit that a third wrecker truck had been summoned to tow away the damaged delivery truck. Tippit walked back to Frazier's car.

He walked around the wrecked car, perusing its overall condition for his accident report. J.D. looked in the back seat. There on the floor was a bolt action rifle with a telescopic sight sticking out of some brown wrapping paper. Tippit told the wrecker driver not to touch anything and to tow the car to the police impound yard, not to the wrecker's repair garage.

Tippit radioed his shift sergeant and updated him on the status of the accident. He informed the sergeant about the discovery of the rifle in the car. Even though this was Texas, fortress of the 2nd Amendment, something didn't feel right.

§

The ambulance containing Wesley Frazier and Lee Harvey Oswald took about 10 minutes to travel to Parkland Memorial Hospital. Oswald was taken to the Emergency Room. He was pronounced dead on arrival. The preliminary cause of death was recorded as blunt head trauma. As it was an accidental death, a formal autopsy would have to be performed.

Frazier was diagnosed with a possible concussion but no other severe injuries. He was shaken and somewhat dazed but conscious. Frazier was able to make a statement to an attending police officer. As he knew Oswald personally, Frazier was able to provide Oswald's next-of-kin information as well as employer information.

The attending policeman telephoned the Irving, Texas police department so Marina Oswald could be contacted about Lee's death.

Frazier was able to contact his wife, who later came to the hospital to pick him up. After a short time of observation, Frazier was released with directions to follow-up with his own physician.

The second ambulance containing Jack Ruby arrived at Parkland some 15 minutes after the first ambulance. Ruby was given a thorough evaluation. Other than a slight bump on the head, he appeared to be in good health. Jack was more concerned about the status of his dog and his briefcase of cash receipts from the Vegas Club. Both the dog and the briefcase had made the trip to the hospital in the same ambulance. Ruby told the medical attendants he still wanted to get back downtown to view the President's parade. He was not happy when the attending police officer informed him that he would, at the least, receive a citation for reckless driving.

Jack's immediate response being, "We'll see about that!"

After completing a police report at the hospital, Ruby was released along with his dog and briefcase. He called for a taxi. There was still time to get the money into the office safe and then go and observe the presidential motorcade.

§

Ron Truly, building manager for the Texas Schoolbook Depository, hung up the phone. Wesley Frazier had called him from home, informing Ron of the earlier auto accident and Lee Oswald's resulting death.

Ron shook his head. Lee had only worked there a little over a month. Ron thought Lee was a good worker; a little bit moody at times but he got the job done. Ron was grateful that Wesley was unhurt. He went to inform the other employees of the situation. Besides, most people were excited about the President's motorcade passing directly in front of their building that day.

Later in the day around 12:30 pm, the presidential motorcade came down Main Street and turned right onto Houston Street for one block. The presidential limousine then proceeded to take a left onto Elm Street, slowly passing the Texas Schoolbook Depository.

It was a clear, sunny day. Enthusiastic crowds had cheered the President and Jackie Kennedy throughout the entire parade route. Local businessman Abraham Zapruder had positioned himself down the street from the Depository building, hoping to get a clear view of the passing motorcade to film with his Bell & Howell home movie camera.

As his wife steadied him, Zapruder filmed the passing presidential limousine, feeling he could almost touch the smiling JFK and his beautiful wife Jackie, in her pretty pink outfit, waving to the crowd.

After the motorcade passed, Zapruder turned to his wife and excitedly exclaimed, "Wasn't that extraordinary! I really got some great footage. I can't wait to see it."

§

The motorcade then drove onto the Dallas Trade Mart. President Kennedy gave a short luncheon speech. However, the highlight of the event was when he introduced Jackie to the large attending crowd. The thundering ovation for Jackie drowned out any subsequent applause for the President.

After the Trade Mart luncheon, the presidential limousine proceeded to Loves Field. The President's entourage boarded Air Force One for an uneventful return flight to Washington D.C.

During the flight back, Kenny O'Donnell reviewed the trip with President Kennedy. "Well, Mr. President, that went very well."

JFK smiled, "Maybe we should get Jackie to run for President. If she can charm Texas, she'd be a lock to win."

Both O'Donnell and the President laughed loudly.

The End

Alan Youmans is retired and lives with his wife Julene in Freeport, Illinois. He is the author of numerous short stories and of *A Rambling Assortment of Writings* and of 24242 *Word Medley*.

The Squirrels in Town

by Mike Bayles

Jeanie spent her early morning spreading mulch around the base of the tree where the flowers were growing. Her knees hurt while she worked, but she wanted to get her yard in shape. The spring air in the morning was fresh, and she hoped to get much done before she had to make her father lunch. Songs of birds filled the air. She glanced at a cluster of brown squirrels in her yard, and shook her head, wondering whether there were more squirrels today than the day before. She grabbed her rake and spread the mulch. When she turned around they were gone. She continued working, singing to herself.

A gray-haired woman walking with a cane came from the house next door and stood at the edge of the yard. Jeanie felt her stare and asked, "Can I help you?"

Jeanie swore that people had been watching since she had moved back to town, ten months earlier.

The woman cleared her throat and asked, "Are those wicker chairs in back antiques?"

"What?"

"I said, are they antiques?"

Although her father had told her not to worry, Jeanie felt uneasy about returning to her hometown after her divorce. High school friends treated her as if she were a stranger, unwilling to forgive her absence of twenty years. Coming back, she noticed that the town hadn't changed, except for the new strip mall by the interstate, and that the old friends she'd seen hadn't changed, either. She noticed that the neighbors kept to themselves, when all she wanted was an invitation for a cup of coffee.

"No, they aren't. I just got them at a store in the city."

Jeanie shook her head in dismay, realizing that her neighbor had gone in back and looked through the screens of her sun porch.

"You looked?"

"Just curious."

She introduced herself to the neighbor, who said that her name was Betty. Betty said that she and her husband, Joe, a retired jeweler, had lived there the last five years. Jeanie reached to offer a handshake, but her neighbor turned and walked away. Joe was waiting by his car.

The town siren sounded at noon. The squirrels ran across her yard. They ran up trees and sat on branches, watching her. When the siren stopped, her neighborhood fell into an uneasy silence. Jeanie set down her rake, and walked to her father's house, just a block away.

"Remember this is a good town," he had said, when she complained about people ignoring her. He patted her on the back and said, "Give it time."

"But when?" She sighed and went to cook his lunch. As his oldest child, the duties of helping him fell upon her. She'd serve him lunch and wash the dishes, and leave before Mary, his new wife and her step mother, would get home. "There are so many squirrels in town," she said.

"Those rascals." He laughed until he had a coughing fit.

A church bell rang, announcing the noon hour.

She thought of the small town and its self-proclaimed virtues. It claimed more churches than bars. She thought about how people even at her church hadn't invited her for coffee.

"They've got their own families." He closed his eyes.

Over the past three weeks, her father had developed a cough, and he spent much of the day sleeping. She noticed while heating a can of soup that he was gazing outside the living room window and crying. She rested her hand on his shoulder and asked him why. For the first time she noticed wrinkles that creased his face. "I'm just a little tired," he said.

She held his hand, and it was cold.

She sat at the table and watched him eat, taking away the dish when his eyelids drooped. She grabbed a blanket from a closet and draped it across his chest. He whispered, "Don't let the squirrels bother you."

"Everybody thinks I'm crazy."

"You're just imagining it." He shook his head.

When she got back home, they were back in her yard, and they chattered at her. They were running across an overhead power line. They were hopping in the air to do squirrel aerobatics. They were either gray or brown, but the brown squirrels, she feared were the most trouble. They stared at her as she planted another shrub.

She looked out the window before going to bed, and they were still there under the yellow glow of a street light. Two of them fought over a scrap of bread.

The next day when Jeanie stepped outside, Betty was seated on her porch, watching. Birds were singing, and a squirrel ran across a power line over the street. She pointed at the squirrel and yelled, "There are more out here." Without a word, Betty stepped into her house. Jeanie hopped onto her lawn tractor, and it sputtered over the yard, while squirrels in trees watched. *It takes a lot of effort to get along,* her father once said.

So the next day, she took out a dish of birdseed, and set it at the edge of the yard, to make peace. She went inside to take a phone call, and when she returned, squirrels surrounded the dish. She grabbed a pair of gloves, and went into the back yard to pull weeds. The overhead sun was bright. Sweat stung her eyes on the sultry day. She heard a noise, and turned around to see the squirrels behind her. When she served her father lunch, she said, "Those little fellows are getting awfully brave."

"You've got to stop this obsession. People in town are talking about you." He doubled over with a cough, and she helped him to bed. She touched his forehead, and it was burning. She frowned, but he sent her on her way. "I'll call you if I need anything," he said.

The squirrels were waiting on her front lawn. She blinked and wondered if even more had come. After finishing her errands, she drove past her father's house, noticing that Mary was there. She stepped on the gas, knowing that Mary didn't want to see her. Exhausted, she decided to go to the diner to eat.

People were laughing when she stepped through the front door. They glanced at her and stopped. A waitress led her to a corner booth, where she sat alone. A retired farmer seated with his wife and then, a minister of her church, who was sitting alone, glanced at her. The minister, himself divorced, shook his head. Even he had been too busy for her.

She looked at him, and remembered the gossip told after *his* divorce.

A squirrel on a drooping branch chattered at her, and she chattered back. The waitress shook her head and left a menu. Jeannie pointed at the window, but the waitress ignored her.

A bird took off from a branch. It was free.

The next morning the squirrels were waiting as she set out a fresh dish of bird seeds. They covered half the yard and chattered among themselves. The grass glistened from the night's rain, and she took in a deep breath of fresh air. A faint crescent moon hung in the sky. As she planted flowers, a car stopped. A reporter held out his camera. She brushed a strand of hair away from her eyes and smiled. "I'm sorry I'm such a mess," she said.

Ignoring her, he pointed the camera at the squirrels, snapped three photos and left. The town siren sounded, and she glanced at her watch. The neighbors got in their car and drove away. They passed her without a glance. A squirrel clung to a branched at it waved with the breeze. She said, "You understand."

It chattered at her. It ran down the trunk of the tree and ran across the street. She smiled, knowing it would come back.

She went to her father's house, and he was lying on the couch. The air was still, and the house was silent. Her head hurt, but she forced a smile. "At least the squirrels like me."

She opened a curtain. Sunlight fell upon him, to show his face drained of color. His breathing came in gasps. He went into a violent coughing spell. When it stopped, he said, "Call, call Mary," and closed his eyes. He took a final breath, and his arm dropped to his side.

With a gentle touch, she closed his eyes. His face wore a stoic expression, and she wondered if he was proud of her. He hadn't told her. She rested her hand on his shoulder and stood next to him, until her step mother arrived. They offered each other a brief greeting, and without another word, Jeanie went home.

Jeanie sighed and sat alone on her front porch steps. The sun hid behind passing clouds, but the neighborhood was alive with a chorus of birds, and the chatter of squirrels. They ran around her yard, occasionally pausing to look at her. *Child's play,* she thought, but with sore knees, she felt her age.

The End

Mike Bayles is a widely-published fiction writer and poet. The characters in his short stories are slightly misfit people who are trying to belong. Short story publishing credits include *The Rockford Review, Feelings of the Heart* and *Out Loud Anthology*. He is the author of three books of poetry: *The Harbor I Seek, The Rabbit House* and *Threshold*.

𝔄 Smile for the Fry Cook

by Connie Kallback

Breakfast customers would soon arrive to order eggs sunny side up or over easy with ham or sausage. Sherman had a long-standing special on those items. He didn't mind the breakfast crowd because it meant mostly fast frying on the grill, and Mae, an efficient waitress, knew automatically what to do. An easy banter during the morning rush kept them working smoothly together.

A lilting voice at the counter urged him to hobble out to see who Mae might be setting up to coffee. Lucille, the attractive middle-age woman who sold cosmetics at the drug store two blocks down, stirred in cream until the brew took on a caramel color. Sherman had never seen her in the diner until today. He wiped his hands on his apron. "Morning, M'am."

She looked up and gave him a genuine smile. "Hello."

He wanted to stay longer gazing at her, but since he had nothing to say and didn't want to make her uncomfortable, he disappeared into the kitchen again where he puttered around, listening to the women talking.

"You like working here, Mae?" Lucille was speaking.

"Oh sure. Been her for so many years now. Don't think I'd know how to do anything else."

"You get tips, too?"

"Yeah. Nothing earth shaking, you know. Enough to keep me going. Don›t you like it in cosmetics?»

"It's O.K. Can be slow. If I got tips, I'd be dragging in quite a bit more. That'd be nice."

Sherman remembered Lucille's smile after she left. It didn't have a trace of disgust or pity like the gawking from people passing in the street when they saw his bent, shriveled leg and the hump emphasizing his right shoulder. His left shoulder sloped downward, giving him a lopsided profile. It seemed as if she truly hadn't noticed. People said he had a handsome enough face, even though he wasn't as young as he used to be.

"Hey, Sherm! Where's that special?" Emmett, the guy who drove Hollander's wholesale produce truck, usually enjoyed teasing Sherman during his breakfast.

"I've got that special, all right. It's been sittin' here half an hour waitin' for you. Hope you like your eggs cold."

"The only way to eat 'em!"

They exchanged a high sign, unique to the two of them.

Sherman hiked himself onto a tall stool on the serving side of the counter to keep company with the only remaining customer. He had heard Mae more than once tell people she thought Sherman slept standing up because he seemed to be always on his feet. He knew she said it to make people think of him as constantly active. In truth, he needed this stool at the counter and another in the kitchen by the grill.

Between mouthfuls, Emmett said, "I saw that gal, Lucille, leaving your place when I stopped at the light earlier. Usually don't see her here." He took a swig of coffee. "Couldn't believe the heavy make-up she was wearing."

Sherman's smile drooped. "She didn't have too much make-up."

Sure as shootin' she did. What's the matter? You gone blind?"

"I saw her up close. Didn't look so bad to me."

"Well if you aren't blind then, you must be in love with her." He bellowed and slapped the counter.

"I don't have time to fool around. Got to cut vegetables for the soup."

Emmett blinked at the retreating, misshapen form. "Mae, what's eating him today? Don't know when I've see him like that. He's usually so cheerful."

She shrugged. "Seemed fine this morning."

§

Mae waited on newcomers while Sherman tended the grill, thinking about the women's conversation at the counter. How would Lucille like to work in the diner? He could offer her more money than the drug store, and she could get tips, too, especially if he let her wait on the booths. Of course, Mae might not be too happy about that. It seemed to him she had been a bit lax here lately, though. Keep her on her toes by giving her some competition. If she didn't like it, maybe she'd take the hint and quit.

He glanced around at the diner's conspicuously less modern interior than the drug store. His father had bought the refurbished railroad car before the war and gotten a deal on a small lot, deeper than it was wide, in the center of town. The lot's small frontage required positioning the dining car at an angle, the only way to accommodate it. One corner jutted out nearly to the edge of the sidewalk. His father thought the arrangement kept it from appearing ordinary. Maybe even a little artistic. In summer, petunias, pansies or other annuals bloomed in a couple of gigantic clay flower pots to help fill in the empty triangle. A wooden turkey replaced them in November, and a Christmas tree in December.

Sherman had been fascinated as a little kid to think his parents spent their days working in a genuine rail car. In those years he played in the three-sided yard in the back and pretended to be the engineer driving the train. In his mind the waitress brought meals to sustain him as he roared through town after town, tooting the horn capriciously and waving wildly at passers-by.

Most of the time, the waitress took the form of his mother – a frail, sad woman who let her thin brown hair hang down beside bangs cut straight across her forehead. She died from a ruptured appendix after his thirteenth birthday. During a good part of those years, she dragged him from one doctor to another to see what they could do about his leg and shoulder. His father had a different solution. He said Sherman should accept his physical appearance by practicing to be stronger and smarter than other people.

In high school, Sherman started pulling regular shifts, working at the diner while the boys who had just graduated went overseas to fight. His handicap kept him at home where he eventually learned about the diner's finances and the buying of food and supplies.

His father retired ten years ago. Four months later, he died in his sleep. A heart attack, they said.

The modernizing of the diner, a constant argument between the two parents, never happened the way his father had imagined. All those doctors charged a lot of money and were never able to do anything anyway. Why *not* fix up the diner to attract more business? But after his wife's death, his father couldn't bear the thought of changing it in any way because she might not have approved.

Stores on both sides had crowded so close, the diner seemed hardly visible anymore. Sherman, answering only to himself, contracted for a triangular extension to the building to bring its front parallel to the sidewalk. New aluminum siding gave the entire facade a sleeker look. His only extravagance came in the form of neon lights buzzing out, "Yorkville Diner." The mortgage he'd taken on his parents' house for the construction didn't provide enough funds to further update the diner's insides.

He scrutinized the remaining evidence of its 1930s vintage. The walls covered with a linoleum type of material had become cracked and old. Long ago he had attached strips of contact wallpaper in a few places. Now it, too, pulled at the edges. He could put up new wallpaper himself or check at the hardware store to see whether paint or another type of wall covering would work. The big round Deco-style mirror, the only embellishment, peered out on diners from the far end.

The tables, new during the construction, still boosted his pride. The floor remained in decent shape. Nothing that a good polishing couldn't fix. He took a dry mop from around the corner and swirled it down the aisle and under the tables. "You know, this place hasn't had a good cleaning in a long time."

Mae raised her eyebrows.

"See if you can shine up that mirror while nobody's here, will you, Mae? And the counter top. We've got to bring back the old gleam."

"Okay. Whatever you want. You're the boss." Opening the cleaning cupboard, she said, "You sure you didn't fall on your head?"

"Have your laugh if you want. Nobody's gonna recognize this place after we're done. It'll sparkle!"

§

Sherman could hardly sleep that night for thinking of Lucille. He had to be casual about approaching her. People might think it strange if he joined her for coffee in one of the booths. He himself sat in a booth only rarely and always alone.

If Lucille didn't come back into the diner the next day, he'd give her a week and then go down to the drugstore to see her. He didn't want to seem obvious about anything, especially to Mae, or Emmett.

He spent a little extra time the next morning getting ready for work and used the special after-shave lotion Mae had given him for Christmas. He didn't worry that she might wonder why he decided to wear it now.

Lucille didn't show. Sherman went home feeling depressed.

The next day before most of the breakfast regulars showed up, he heard her voice.

"You're here again, huh?" Mae said, surprise edging her voice. "Must have been some good cup of coffee I made you the other day."

Sherman wanted to step into the serving area right away, but he needed a task to get Mae away from there. An errand to the post office would do it. He listened a moment longer.

"Not the best cup of coffee I ever had . . ." Lucille's voice became soft and giggly.

A good sign. She hadn't come there just for the coffee. In a matter of seconds he practiced his speech to her and felt strangely in control.

A loud laugh snorted from the counter.

He paused at the doorway in time to see Mae trying to shush the other woman.

"And the hump! I had to come back again to see if it's for real."

Laughter slipped from Mae before she got control of herself. "He's a prince of a guy when you get to know him."

Sherman slowly inched his way back into the kitchen's privacy. *You've got to accept yourself the way you are.* A reminder from his father. When a boy laughed at him, his father said, *Give it to him, Sherm. You're tougher than he is.*

If Lucille were a man, he'd give her such a shot . . . . But she wasn't a man. His father never taught him how to handle these situations.

The cash register rang open. He stepped to the doorway and said in the coolest voice he could manage, "Mae, tell her the coffee's on me."

The End

Connie Kallback, former managing editor of business publications at McGraw-Hill, Prentice Hall, and acquisitions at CPP, Inc., lives in North Carolina with her husband. Her work has recently appeared in *Foliate Oak, Gravel, Lowestoft Chronicle* and *The Rockford Review.*

Lady Luck

by Joy Rewold Schneider

Walking into a casino was like entering an adult after-hour theme park, but entering a Las Vegas casino was the ultimate fantasyland! At this casino, Julius Caesar hailed us at the front door. Once inside, more marbled classical statues and columns accentuated the Greco-Roman theme playground. Everywhere I looked there were opportunities to gamble, with beautiful female 'slaves' in mini-tunics and high-heeled Roman-style sandals serving free cocktails to encourage the flow of betting. Caesars Palace's mesmerizing patterned carpet, its low ceilings, and mellow chandelier lighting immediately lured me into its gaming colosseum.

Strolling by carousels of slot machines with bells ringing, strobe-like lights flashing, and wheels spinning made me feel like everyone was winning –so we could too! Dad, Grandma, and I were already in fantastic moods, having just seen Celine Dion's Show! Besides, Dad was wearing his lucky gold Jewish Chai, Grandma had her player's card attached to her own beloved lavaliere around her neck, and I was feeling special in my little black dress.

"This Cleopatra slot machine should help me conquer the Roman Empire's treasury. You know, Cleopatra was a famous Roman goddess," Grandma said.

"Bubbe, you mean Egyptian ruler," I said.

"That's even a better reason why she'd like to take money out of this Roman casino," Grandma responded, as she plumped herself into the chair and pushed her player's card into the slot machine.

"Okay, Mom. You know where to find us," Dad said. "Come on, Nancy, you're my lucky charm." Taking my right elbow, he led me deeper into the heart of the casino.

When we arrived at the craps tables, Dad shopped for a hot dice game. All the tables were crowded, but that didn't stop him from squeezing us into one. "This one feels lucky, and with you by my side, I can't lose," he said. Then he kissed me on the cheek and whispered, "Besides, it will be exciting to watch the big whale with the large bankroll at the other end of the table."

"Yeah, let's conquer Caesar," I said, laughing. Then I looked around the table for the high roller Dad was talking about. The bathtub-shaped table was surrounded by an assortment of people. Some were standing tall waiting for the game to continue, while others were leaning over positioning their chips on the marked green felt, trying to get their last minute bets placed. The 'whale,' as dad called him, was diagonal from us at the far end of the tub. A large man with a large head, his right hand was resting on the bare shoulders of an attractive lady, while the other hand was embracing a cocktail. The lady caught me staring and nodded at me. I smiled back and quickly turned my attention to the cloth 'layout' where all the chips were deposited.

The betting areas on the 'layout' were the same at both ends of the table with additional proposition bets in the middle for all to use, so that the players didn't have to reach too far into the tub to place their bets. The 'On' button or marker was showing on the table, meaning a point had been established. The shooter was throwing for a nine.

"Dice are coming out. No more bets," cried the stickman, as he raised his long wooden stick. "Seven. Craps," he called when the shooter crapped out.

With a fresh round to begin, it was Dad's chance to join in the game. He dropped a pile of bills on the table. "Coloring-in," cried the base dealer across from us. The boxman, seated behind stacks of casino chips and between the two base dealers, counted the bills and exchanged them for one thousand dollars worth of chips. Dad placed two $25 green chips on the 'Come' and then organized the rest of his chips on the rail in front of him according to denominations. Now, we were ready for some hot action.

The new shooter selected two dice and quickly tossed them against the textured back wall of the table. "Six, easy six," the stickman yelled, as he collected the cubes showing two dots on one and four dots on the other. The stickman flipped the marker over to the 'On' side and placed it on the number six. Dad bet on the shooter to make the point, even wagering ten dollars on the hard six, while placing bets on all the inside numbers.

"Dice coming out," cried the stickman, as the young hurler was blowing on the dice for good luck. "Eight, soft eight," shouted the stickman, as he again collected the dice in his elongated hook.

"Press the eight," my dad said, parlaying his original wager when the nearest dealer tried to give him his payout.

"I wanna pass the dice now that I'm up," said the inexperienced shooter, who had been making sucker bets on the numbers in the middle of the table when we first arrived.

"Hey kid, here's something to keep you going," the high roller shouted, tossing a $100 black chip. "Now, stop making those damn sucker bets and let that all ride on the 'Pass line'," he roared, downing his drink.

"Gee, thanks! Okay, the free chip goes on the 'Pass line'. Come on Lady Luck!" the young man said, picking up the dice again.

"Hands high, let's fly," shouted the stickman, looking around the crowded table.

"Yo, six," Dad shouted like a cheerleader, calling for the current point along with everyone else as the dice flew through the air.

Once the dice bounded off the far wall of the table onto the felt, everyone roared as two threes were face up. Dad gave me a big smooch on the cheek. "33, winner 6! Came hard. Shooter makes his point the hard way," yelled the stickman. With that, the kid ran around the table and hugged the whale.

"Here, kid, do it again," the superstitious big shot said, handing over another black chip.

But in an adrenaline rush, the kid accidentally threw the dice so hard they bounced off the table.

"Same dice!" yelled the whaler, with a fresh cocktail in his one hand and the other still around his lady.

With that, the kid nodded, and the stickman passed the youngster the retrieved dice and announced, "Come out roll."

Dad was up hundreds but lost some of that on the next toss of the dice when the kid crapped out and then cashed out.

The game continued as the dice shifted to the next player who was an Asian gentleman. He was able to hit some of our numbers again, only to lose those chips and more in the next couple of throws. I felt like I was on a roller coaster. I was anxiously holding my breath, while my dad continued to cheer for the points along with the whale. With a little help from his liquor, Dad had become the whaler's best friend. In fact, they were on a first name basis along with some of the other players at the table.

"Hey Sid, who's your girlfriend there?" Dick, the whaler, asked Dad.

"She's my daughter, Nancy."

"Sure she is, just like this one is my niece," he yelled back, smacking his lady on the butt.

"No really. I'm his nurse too," I said, playing with the whaler.

"Nurse Nancy, how cute. Can I be sick too?" Dick asked.

"Don't get too sick, I've only been out-of-school for six months," I said with a laugh, as a new round began.

The dice passed and so did the time, yet I had no idea what time it really was because there were no clocks, windows or cell phone usage in our area. I was sure that time was slipping deep into the night, but Dad and his playmates didn't appear to notice. Almost everyone at the table was in a very jovial mood including the dealers.

There was great camaraderie because most of the players had the same bets on the line, except for the somber middle aged man next to me. This grim man was playing the 'darkside', and so the other players at the table had nicknamed him Darth Vader. Vader was betting against the shooter on the 'Don't Pass' line, which was really against us too. He was smoking cigarette after cigarette, lighting the next one off the butt of the last. The smoke was getting in my eyes and the nurse in me spoke up, "Boy, you sure are smoking a lot. How many packs a day do you smoke?"

"I don't know about five or six. I don't keep track," he replied.

"Gee, that must burn a hole in your gambling money," I said, as Vader shrugged his shoulders. Then, I continued, "Aren't you afraid it's bad for your health?"

"Well, Darth Vader, if you do have a heart attack, you have a nurse right next to you who can give you mouth-to-mouth," Dick whaled from the far end of the table.

"Listen. My mother is ninety, and she smokes seven packs a day and has never been sick a day in her life," Vader boasted to everyone.

Now everyone was giving Vader the evil eye. "What?" Vader asked the crowd. "Oh, you are all afraid of the word seven? I've been rooting for that number all night," he bragged.

Now his playmates were about to fight him so I quickly tried to end the exchange. "Well, I hope you are just as lucky," I replied, as I looked away, knowing the odds were against him.

"Luck doesn't have anything to do with it," he snapped back.

Dad, listening to the conversation, piped in, "It's all about luck. You gotta always believe in the Lady. For life is like a crap shoot, so you should never cross Lady Luck."

"I don't know and I don't care. I'm just sticking around here until I lose these last few chips," Vader said.

Shaking his head, Dad turned back to the game. Trying to change the mood, he shouted, "Come on, shooter, fire away!"

Dick joined in, "Yeah, show Vader the light!"

Just then the shooter threw the dice. He made another point, taking the smoker's last chips. The smoker was snuffed out as the rest of the table cheered. As Dad and I hugged in celebration, Dad whispered in my ear, "Well, at least he's only been jinxing himself all night."

"Waitress, I'll have another drink. Hey, anybody else want anything? I'm buying," whaled Moby Dick, as he toasted his playmates.

"Hey, what's going on? I could hear you guys screaming from across the room," Grandma said, squeezing in between Dad and me.

"We're having a hell of a winning streak," Dad said.

"Oh, good. I need more money. Cleopatra killed me," Grandma said.

"I could've told you that you were committing suicide," Dad replied. "Craps is the only game in here that gives you a chance to survive because it gives you the best odds."

"Oh, Nancy, aren't you tired of standing here? Why don't you come play slots with me?" Grandma asked.

"No, she can't leave now. I'm winning!" Dad said, grabbing my hand.

"Maybe later, Bubbe," I said, giving her a weak smile.

"Okay, but I can't stand here with my stupid back. I'm going to find a hot man, I mean slot," Grandma corrected, covering her mouth with her right hand.

"Here's one," Dick yelled, planting a big kiss on his girl's lips. All the players laughed along with Dick as Grandma grabbed a handful of chips and backed out.

When the hot shooter eventually sevened out, my bladder was also about to crap out. "Dad, I'm running to the bathroom," I whispered.

He just nodded, as he continued to watch the game. Dad was up thousands of dollars, and all his chips couldn't fit on his rack. So he set stacks of $5 red, $25 green, and $100 black chips on the felt in front of him and next to his current payout to exchange them for larger denominations.

"Coloring-in" cried our dealer, as he began counting and stacking them in groups.

With all the commotion, I didn't want to bother Dad with directions to the bathroom. Besides I couldn't hold it any longer. With all my attention on my full bladder, I walked around the casino feeling like I was in a giant maze. Traveling away from our craps table, past other dice tables, through black jack tables, and around roulette tables into a sea of slot machines; I felt like I was going in circles. It seemed that with every turn there was another gaming obstacle between me and finding the bathroom.

Finally, five pounds lighter, I walked out of the bathroom. Thinking it was a good time to try and find Grandma, I was surprised to spot her right away. She was playing a Wheel of Fortune slot machine and muttering to herself in Yiddish.

"Hi, Bubbe. How's it going?" I asked.

"*Oy vey!* This machine is a *gonif*. It keeps stealing all my money," she said, shaking her finger at it.

"I'm sure you'll do better," I consoled her, thinking Dad would hate me for giving Grandma false hope.

"I'm getting a *luch* in my head from this thing," she said, as she slapped the top of her head with her palm.

Then, as Grandma continued to lose more credits in the machine, I saw firsthand why Dad called it the 'one-armed bandit'. "No, Bubbe, you're not getting a hole in your head. You're only getting a hole in your purse!"

"Oh, nonsense, anyway, this is your Dad's wallet," she said laughing. "By the way, will you play this for me while I go to the bathroom? I've had to stay near the bathroom because I can't seem to hold my bladder anymore," Grandma said, as she dashed for the bathroom.

Running back out of the bathroom, Grandma shouted, "I kept hearing a Wheel of Fortune machine going off. Was that you getting all those spins?"

"Yeah, I've been lucky," I said.

"Great. Keep it up. It seems like I've been waiting all night to win a spin," Grandma said.

"No, I can't. I promised Dad I'd come right back. You know how superstitious he is," I said.

"Yeah, he's like his Dad, may he rest in peace," Grandma said, taking over the hot seat and waving me off.

When I finally found my way back to Dad, he said, "Boy, am I glad you're back. The game has really stalled."

"I stopped to check on Grandma," I said.

"Was she in the café eating?" Dad asked.

"No, not yet. She was still at the slots," I replied.

Returning to the craps table was like waiting in line to be served a delicious chocolate cupcake while you watch other shooters smacking their lips on the dark chocolate frosting. One shooter after another took turns firing the dice, as the dice slowly rotated clockwise around the table, until it was finally our turn for dessert! The stickman presented Dad with five dice. Dad selected two and the stickman collected the other three. Dad doubled his usual coming out bet and gave me a big grin. He was about to take control of the dice, to determine his own fate, and get a sweet taste of the action, which he always said was the biggest thrill at the table.

Dad even had his own lucky shooter ritual. Using one hand, he set the dice the hard way with fives on top, glued them together between his thumb and index finger and threw them lightly. The dice touched and bounced off the back wall of the table, rolling over and over until they landed.

"Yo-leven. Natural winner," cried the stickman, gathering up the displayed five and six dice with his stick.

With that, Dad gave me a fireworks fist bump and cried, "Boom!" All the players with chips on the 'Pass Line' cheered as the dealers made their payouts.

The stickman passed Dad his dice again. Dad arranged them as before with the fives showing and then threw them.

"Easy eight, point is eight," the stickman announced, as he positioned the 'On' puck over the eight.

The dealer placed bets on the table per Dad's instruction including covering the hard eight, while Dad made additional bets behind the pass line to increase his odds. With the two fives smiling up at him again, Dad tossed the dice. He threw a nine. More cheers circled the table. Dad pressed his bets with his winnings. The table was covered already with a buffet of chips when the drunk whale threw more chips around like pieces of bread and yelled, "Okay, Let'em roll!"

Then Dad threw an easy six, then a three, and so on until he hit the eight with a three and a five! The players around the table went wild, clapping and cheering. I was jumping up and down. Dad was hot and on a winning streak, and we all could feel it –even the dealers!

"Coming out. Another point comin," said the stickman. "Hard ten. Puppy paws," he shouted over the roar of the players, as Dad's two lucky fives lay face up on the table.

"Keep them coming," shouted Moby Dick.

Dad tossed more chips on the table and instructed the dealer, "Bet those all the hard ways. And here's a hardway for the dealers too." He added, placing a separate bet for the dealers using additional chips.

"Hot roll comin," the stickman rooted. "THREE, acey deucey!" cried the stickman. "Still looking for a ten," he announced, as he passed the dice back to Dad.

It was like the man had ordered it because 'Puppy paws' appeared! Again the table went wild. Dad's playmates were giving him pats on his back and high fives, as the dealers thanked Dad for their winning tip.

"Good luck, Sid," the stickman said, passing Dad the dice to start a new round. "Come out roll.... easy four. Point is four" continued the stickman, moving the point puck to four.

Dad maxed out his bets again, set the dice as usual, and tossed them, crying; "Yo –four!"

Just then Grandma grabbed my arm, and pulled me out of the game.

"There's a person in the café who is choking," she screamed over the roar of the table. Never letting my hand go, she dragged me to the café. "There," she pointed.

I quickly approached an elderly man, who had both hands clutching his throat. "Are you choking?" I asked. He nodded yes, as his lips were turning blue. "Would you like me to help you?" He immediately nodded affirmative again. "Okay, I'm going to do a Heimlick maneuver, which is an abdominal thrust procedure," I told him.

Standing behind the man, I put my arms around his waist overlapping my right fist with my left hand just below his breastbone. "Okay, lean forward and try and relax," I instructed. I forced my double fist backward into his stomach with a hard, upward thrust. A piece of hot dog flew across the table. The man coughed and wiggled out of my arms as he coughed again.

"Are you okay now?" I asked. He nodded, taking a sip of water.

"Boy, am I glad I was having dinner with your grandma," the man said.

"Yeah, I told you she was a nurse," Grandma said.

"So, Nancy, want to join us for some food? Julius was treating me, and I'm sure he would treat you too. That is," Grandma said, turning back to Julius, "if you still want to eat."

"Sure, nothing has made it to my stomach yet. Please have a seat," Julius said, pulling out a chair.

"Okay, I feel I earned a reward, and I've been craving a chocolate dessert all night," I said. "By the way, your last name isn't Caesar is it?" I teased him.

"Oh, no," he said laughing. "It's Stein."

Just then, Dad appeared. "I knew I'd find you two here. What happened to you?" he asked me, and then continued: "I had hundreds of dollars on the table when you suddenly left, and then I crapped out."

"Oh, your daughter just saved my life," Julius piped in.

"Yeah, Julius and I were enjoying a nice dinner when he choked on his hot dog. I knew Nancy would know what to do, so I got her," Grandma added.

"Yeah, Nancy brings everyone and everything she touches good luck. Especially in a casino!" Dad said, giving me a big kiss on my cheek. "So, do you have room for one more?" he asked. "I'm sure I can get my casino host to comp our entire bill after all the action I gave the casino tonight. And food always tastes better when it's free!"

I chimed right in, "Great! I'm going to order every chocolate dessert on the menu. This really is my lucky night!"

The End

Joy Rewold Schneider is a retired nurse. She received her M.S.N. from the University of Miami, and has published several articles in professional nursing journals. Currently, she and her husband live in Pompano Beach, Florida where she continues to write for fun.

Words Used at the Craps Tables

Action: the total amount of money the shooter bets

Bank: the casino's money used by the dealer to pay winning bets

Big 6: an even money bet (or flat bet) that a 6 will be rolled before a 7

Boxman: the craps table's supervisor, who sits between the two dealers

Box Numbers: the numbers 4, 5, 6, 8, 9, and 10

Cage: the cashier's "window"

Chips: casino betting tokens; red chips are $5, green chips are $25, and black chips are $100

Color Change or Coloring: changing the denomination of a player's chips, say four greens for a black

Come-Out: the very first roll of the dice, either a 7 or 11 called a "natural" (shooter wins); or a 2, 3, or 12 called "craps" (shooter loses); or a 4, 5, 6, 8, 9, or 10 called "the point"

Comp: free (complementary) meals, drinks, etc. given by the casino to favored gamblers

Craps: the game of dice

Crapping Out: throwing, on the first toss, a 2, 3, or 12 (shooter loses)

<u>Easy Way</u>: rolling a 4, 6, 8, or 10 without rolling the pair of numbers that equal any of those numbers; i.e., rolling a 1 and 3 as opposed to two 2s

<u>Field Bet</u>: a one-roll, even money wager that the next roll will yield a 2, 3, 4, 9, 10, 11, or 12; the casino has a big "edge" or advantage on field bets

<u>Hardway</u>: rolling a 4, 6, 8, or 10 by rolling the pair of numbers that equal any of those numbers; i.e., rolling two 2s as opposed to a 1 and a 3

<u>Layout</u>: the surface of the craps table with the various betting words, boxes, bars, etc. printed on it

<u>Making the Point</u>: rolling the point number before rolling a 7 (shooter wins)

<u>Marker</u> or <u>Puck</u>: a special disk conspicuously placed on the layout indicating the point the shooter is rolling for

<u>Marker</u>: also an IOU note

<u>Natural</u>: a 7 or 11 rolled on the first throw (shooter wins)

<u>Odds</u>: the ratio of ways to win over ways to lose; there are four ways to roll a 5 and thirty-two ways to not roll a 5; therefore, the ratio is 4 over 32 or 1 over 8 or 12 ½ %

<u>To Pass</u>: to win; a pass bet is the money the shooter bets prior to the initial roll of the dice and with the intention of rolling a 7 or an 11 or of rolling a point number and then making that point; in contrast, a <u>Don't Pass</u> bet is a bet against the shooter, that he will not make his point but will roll a 7

<u>Pass Line</u>: the area on the layout where the shooter places his wager before his first throw

<u>A Place Bet</u>: a bet made after the first throw that a specific 4, 5, 6, 8, 9, or 10 will be rolled before a 7

<u>Point</u>: a 4, 5, 6, 8, 9, or 10 rolled on the first throw

<u>To Press a Bet</u>: to increase or double an existing bet

<u>Puck</u>: a special disk conspicuously placed on the layout indicating the point the shooter is rolling for

<u>To Punt</u>: to lay a bet against the bank

<u>Sevening Out</u>: rolling a 7 before rolling the point number (shooter loses)

<u>Shooter</u>: the player who throws the two dice; just before throwing, the shooter must make a bet on the table

<u>Stickman</u>: the casino employee who maneuvers the dice over the table with the curved end of a long stick

<u>Table Limit</u>: most casinos require a minimum of $5 for a bet at their craps tables

<u>Yo yo-leven</u>: a way of pronouncing the number 11 in order to distinguish it audibly from the number 7

"𝕭elieve in the 𝕷ady"

The Palm Reader

by Edward Grosek

*H*arry and Stella sat there waiting, letting their eyes roam over the students who were streaming through the University's food court. It was lunch time, and the vast hall and its food concessions and aisles were swelling with students. Boys in shorts walked by, their sox-less feet in sneakers. Girls too, their legs in tight pants. At a table not far from Harry and Stella's, boys in green and white fraternity jackets had gathered. Boisterously, one of them laughed. His fellows joined in, and Stella turned to her husband. "I certainly hope Paul's not one of those loud fraternity types!"

It was late October. Harry and Stella Clark had driven from Pennsylvania to see their daughter and meet her boyfriend Paul. In particular, Stella wanted to assure herself that Marcie, who was in her junior year, had not let herself become attracted to someone who was conceited or show-offish.

That Paul was neither of these nor a 'fraternity type' would very shortly become evident.

All at once a knot of students proceeding in the Clarks' direction came apart, and from within, Marcie appeared. She was walking hesitantly, scanning her eyes from table to table, letting other students pass by her. Stella's face livened. "There's my sweet girl." In the same moment, Marcie spied her parents. She turned her head and spoke to someone behind her, then pushed forward.

In her wake came Paul wearing a pea coat. The coat had wide lapels and was unbuttoned, and about its collar a scarf curled, its ends dangling. From one of the coat's pockets a sheet of paper protruded. Paul's hair was combed but not parted; and upon his nose, which arched with a slight aquilinity, were black-framed glasses. His countenance as a whole conveyed the kindled, expectant spirit of a youth who was about to be presented to a movie star.

At the table, as the two doffed their rucksacks, Marcie introduced Paul Basarabi. She moved to her mother, who was sitting on Harry's left, and kissed her and sat next to her. Harry and Paul greeted each other and shook hands. Paul shrugged out of his coat and draped it over the back of the remaining chair. His rucksack he lowered to the floor and, without interrupting his smile to the Clarks, sat.

"So you two met last semester?"

Harry asked this with a placid fatherly smile. The question was aimed at Paul, but it was Marcie who answered. "In geography class, Daddy." Marcie's lips were modest in size, her complexion free of rouge and lipstick.

Paul turned to Stella. "Mrs. Clark, how long did it take you to drive up here?" His voice was engaging and sonorous but low in volume.

"Almost five hours. Because we stopped for coffee." Just then, Stella noticed the talisman that Paul was wearing, a black and honey-streaked stone suspended from a gold link necklace. She lifted herself from her chair and leaned across the table. "Is that a good luck piece, Paul? An amulet?"

On the stone's façade was carved a man's head. The man's visage was facing out but had only one prodigious off-center right eye. Paul held out the quaint object for Stella and Harry to see. Stella took it and fingered it gingerly and then released it; an examination out of curiosity that would soon divert the talk at the table from the commonplace to the occult.

"It's new. So... I can't tell yet whether its powers are helping me," Paul said; and at this, all four laughed affably.

He grinned to Stella –was he teasing her? Stella's eyebrows ascended and her face brightened. She thought, "He has a nice humor. And there's no cigarette smell on his breath."

Paul's parents are from Romania," said Marcie. "From Transylvania! There're still medieval castles there! With gargoyles and dungeons!" Marcie's voice gushed with excitement.

"Huh! Where Dracula's from," Harry thought.

Marcie went on. "Paul believes that castles could be haunted by souls, maybe, or muses!" She fixed her eyes on Paul.

Her look stirred him, and he pursued the matter. "When I visited Chestnut Hill Cemetery in Exeter, Rhode Island, I was able to study the tombstone of Mercy Brown. She was a proven –"

But as he heard, 'able to study the tombstone,' Harry's skepticism overcame his patience, and he cut in. "What're you studying here, Paul? What do you want to do someday?"

"I want to write… about unexplained reality –as subject matter *in fiction*." He stressed the last two words.

"Paul's looking for story material," Marcie added.

"Story material," Harry repeated to himself.

"I'm majoring in English now. I want to go on and earn a master's degree in journalism."

Harry, with an interrogatory look, said, "And… ?"

"I want to work in the publishing business. So I can publish my stories."

"Stories?"

"Currently I'm just incubating my ideas –"

"And palm reading!" interjected Marcie. "Paul studies palm reading. He read my palm. He saw that I'd had meningitis when I was a girl!"

"Oh, my," sighed Stella, shaken that this half-forgotten incident should be again brought to the surface.

At this last disclosure, Harry's eyes narrowed: could this Paul Basarabi be indoctrinating his daughter?

"Well," Paul faced Marcie, "Marcie, no. What I read from your lines was only –"

"Paul," said Stella, "is this... fortunetelling?"

"It's fantasy!" answered Harry. He wanted to say, "A hoax!"

"But, Daddy," Marcie remonstrated, "isn't that why you read those Fu-Manchu books of yours? Because Fu-Manchu invents all those *fan-tas-tic* poisons and murder devices! Right?"

Harry had within his collection of books a miscellany, perhaps half, of Sax Rohmer's Fu-Manchu mysteries. Someday, he hoped, he could locate and buy the missing titles and display the full series on one of his book shelves.

"I know what you mean," Paul said to Marcie. "Indeed, my great Aunt Anna has a complete –"

"Is this a kind of science?"

"Not yet, Mrs. Clark. You grip and crease your fingers and palms as life affects you. Grooves result."

Stella glanced down at her palms. "Humm."

"They're not really mute. They tell about your past and about your strengths and inclinations. But you see, in order to accredit palmistry to be a true diagnostic –"

"Paul," Stella reached across to him, "read Harry's palm."

"What?!" exclaimed Harry, roused by her words. Tightening his lips into a straight line, he shook his head 'No.'

"Yes!" Marcie was smiling gleefully.

"Mr. Clark is unconvinced –"

"Oh, Harry is just underconvinced!" Stella was feeling, there within the confines of their genial table, a preternatural excitement. "I believe in you, Paul. Harry, put out your hand and let Paul read your fortune."

"I'm not an expert, Mrs. Clark." But in spite of these words, Paul did want to read the writing on Harry's palm, to show off his extraordinary talent. He smiled to Marcie, and she beamed back at him.

In the next few seconds they heard chairs scraping over the hard vinyl flooring, wrapped lunches being unwrapped, joke-making and laughter –the turmoil of the lunch crowd. Harry's wife was showing insistence on her face, and he heard his daughter say, "You'll like this, Daddy!"

"Are you game, Mr. Clark?"

Outnumbered, how could Harry not agree? "Go ahead," he said evenly. He thought, "I'll let you prove the whole thing a fake."

Paul smiled accommodatingly. He took Harry's left hand and placed it palm-side up on the table's surface, where light from the overhead fixtures could illuminate it. Marcie and Stella, fully fascinated, pushed closer to the table; and Paul began.

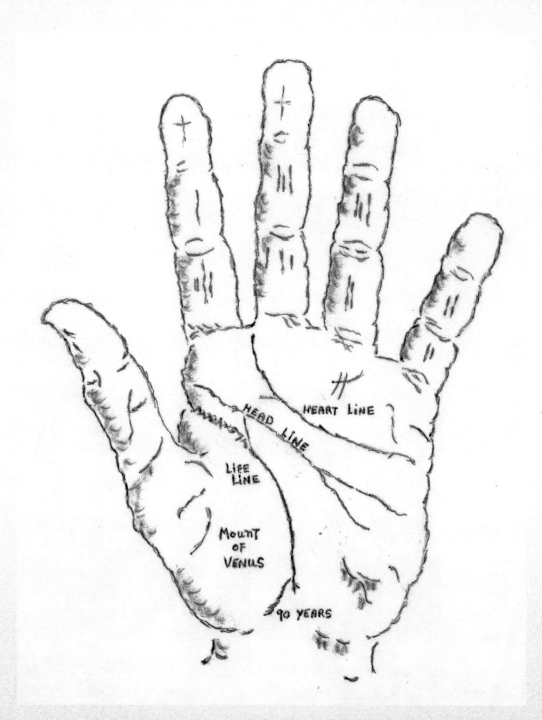

"Here goes." The four looked at the recumbent palm. "Note the long fourth finger. It tells that Mr. Clark is a risk-taker." From his shirt pocket Paul withdrew a pencil and began sketching indicatively over the palm. "Note the crisscrossing of both ingrained lines and fine lines. Mr. Clark knows when to keep a secret!"

Marcie laughed. "See, Daddy!"

Paul identified the major lines of the palm, then ran the pencil over the life line, the pronounced line semi-circling Harry's thumb and its mount. This is the line that dominates the interest of palmists; and upon it, Paul expounded.

"The life line issues from this point between the thumb and the index finger –see? –and travels around the thumb's Mount of Venus to its base. Its length is the length of the person's life. Mr. Clark has a full line. I'd say it denotes ninety years of living."

"Ninety years!" echoed Stella.

"See how it's tattered at its beginning –under the index finger? That's evidence of turbulence in Mr. Clark's childhood." At these words, no one spoke. He pressed Harry's plump Mount of Venus and said that the fleshiness therein indicates a need for collecting things.

Paul bent over the palm, and light from one of the ceiling's pendant lamps reflected on the lenses of his glasses. "Looks like there's a break in the life line –when you were, maybe... ten years old, Mr. Clark?"

"A break?" asked Stella.

"An interruption in the continuity, or an off-shoot."

Harry smiled wanly, enigmatically. Marcie looked from her father to Paul, who continued to search the hand as if he had erred somehow. "A break or bar in the life line," he raised his head, "is revealing. It indicates distress or a scare at that moment in life..."

"What happened to you, Harry?" Stella asked.

"Ten years old, Mr. Clark?" Paul cocked his head inquiringly.

Harry said nothing. The others looked at him. A recess in his memory opened.

That year, that autumn when Harry was ten and a half years old, Bernie Carmen, an older boy at school, appeared at Harry's front door. Bernie's hair was cut short. His mouth widened ravenously when he spoke, and the fingers of his hands terminated in thick pads. It was a Saturday evening after supper. The two boys came down the front steps and onto the sidewalk, and Bernie said, "See this key, Clarkie?" The key he waved at Harry was a security key. "It's the key t'Zap's back door!"

By 'Zap's,' Bernie meant Mr. Zapotocky's grocery store, which was near their school. He went on, bragging. "I went into Zap's t'day for a candy bar. He was stackin' shelves, see. So I reached over the counter and stuck my hand in the drawer. And I grabbed what I could –this key! So I went around the back and tried the back door. It worked!"

Harry looked dumbfounded. Bernie everted his lips derisively at Harry, smirking at him. "We're gonna get his money tonight, *amico*. Y'know Zap's is closed by now. I need a lookout."

"But –"

"See, the money's in his meat locker."

"How d'you know that, Bernie?"

"Everybody's seen Zap go in there for change, Clark!" He poked Harry's chest. "You're gonna watch out the side windows!"

Sure enough, the key unlocked Mr. Zapotocky's rear entrance.

"I'll wait here –"

Again Bernie smirked. Gripping Harry by the shirt collar, he pulled him through the doorway and into the store, then pocketed the key. "The key stays with me, Clark. You stay by those windows!"

Bernie moved quickly to the meat locker, a walk-in freezer for meats and ice cream. The freezer's door opened outward; its latch was a handle on a pivot that, when the freezer was closed, fit firmly into a clamp welded to the door's casing. Bernie yanked the handle up out of the clamp, heaved open the heavy door, and plunged into the frost-filled chamber.

Moments passed. Harry looked about the dim interior of the store, remembering the many times he had come in after school. He felt impatient to leave. Bernie would gloat about this Monday, he knew. Then he heard, "Yeah! I got it, Clark! In this box! Maybe a hun'durt! Cold cash. Cold-as-ice cash!"

The freezer's door hung open. Harry edged closer and looked expressionlessly at its inside surface, which was all one piece, one featureless panel with not even a door-grip fixed onto it.

Suddenly, indifferently, Harry stepped to the door and with all his might swung it shut. Violently it banged into place, and the latch-handle dropped from its upright position into the clamp. Bernie began thumping on the door. Harry heard muffled words, and then he heard –or thought he heard, "You'll get half! You'll get half!"

"You got the key in your pocket," Harry said softly to the voice in the freezer. His lower lip jutted out. "And Zap's is closed on Sundays." Cautiously he turned the knob of the rear door, exited, and pulled the door closed. The beveled tongue of the door lock clicked as it slid into the faceplate.

Harry's entire reminiscence passed through his mind in only seconds. He raised his eyebrows questioningly to Paul, as if he were waiting for Paul to respond to him: it was an old trick.

Paul turned and asked Marcie for her magnifying glass.

"We used it on old maps," Marcie explained to her mother, who nodded in reply.

Paul positioned the glass; and lowering his eyes over it, he peered at the chain of tiny ringlets in Harry's life line. With the pencil, he traced from Harry's middle finger down to the line itself and there, at that point, pressed upon the pencil. His face intensified, for here was a second break.

"According to what I've read so far in my book, this intersection marks your first twenty or twenty-one years of life. There's another break here, Mr. Clark." He paused. "Age twenty? Something at college?"

Stella asked, "What did you do, Harry?"

But again Harry met the questions with blithe silence and with an expression of nonchalance. Again he let himself remember.

That year, his junior year at the University, Harry requested and was approved to live singly, that is, without a roommate, in one of the men's residence buildings. He arrived on Monday, two days preceding the start-up of classes, and began removing his clothes from his suitcases. But at noon he was informed that the University had accepted several late-admission foreign students. Harry would have a roommate after all, an engineering major, in fact.

Immediately, the roommate appeared with his luggage. Introducing himself politely and in what to Harry sounded like colonially-learned English, the newcomer patted Harry on the shoulder and predicted that they both will profit handsomely from their room-sharing.

Abruptly he turned and took as his one of the two as yet empty desks and pulled it over the floor to the window. "I arise at 7 o'clock," he advised Harry.

Then, as if to demonstrate his affluence –or maybe that of his family –he extracted from his belongings a certified check for $8,650, the sum that was required to cover his year's tuition and housing fees. He let Harry examine the check. The line marked 'payee' was left blank, the future engineer explained, because he had been unsure how the University should be formally addressed.

Replacing the check in its envelope, grinning to Harry and taking his arm, he said, "Let us take lunch together, Harry. We'll talk about ourselves. We'll look all over the engineering building and go to the Student Accounts Office."

Harry shrugged. "O.K."

They lunched at the University's cafeteria, wandered about the engineering building, and arrived finally at the Office of Students Accounts, at the window marked 'Payments.' The roommate opened the book he was carrying, in which he had secreted the envelope with the check. The book was empty. As he flipped through it page by page, terror spread unashamedly across his face, for somehow the envelope had fallen out! "My father!" he cried, looking up.

"Quickly!" Harry exclaimed, putting his hand comfortingly on the roommate's shoulder. "You go back to the engineering building. I'll backtrack to the cafeteria. We'll find it!" he declared.

Harry ran back to the cafeteria, to the garbage receptacle they had used. He lifted the lid and clawed through the wet wrappings and coffee cups. He knelt down and looked under all the nearby tables; and underneath the salad counter, he swept his arm. He pressed his face over the narrow space between the wall and the radiator –where he spotted the envelope. "Of course!" The roommate, Harry recalled, had rested the book upright on the radiator for a moment. He snatched up the envelope with its precious content and pushed it inside his shirt.

He rushed to the library, to the reference department's shelves where the telephone directories were kept. Quickly he chose one for a large out-of-state city and with it under his arm, went to the library's typewriting room. There he sat down at one of the typewriters, removed its dust cover, and opened the thick directory to the section where were listed churches by their denominations.

"Here's a good one." Confidently and without glancing about, Harry took out the roommate's check, rolled it onto the typewriter's cylinder, and on the payee's line typed, 'CHURCH OF DEVOTED HOLISTIC FAITH.' On the envelope he typed the name and address of the Church.

With the envelope sealed and hidden inside his shirt, he raced –literally –to the University's bookstore where he bought a postage stamp. Minutes later, the envelope and its sole property, a draft ordering the roommate's bank to pay $8,650 to a church about whose existence the roommate knew nothing, was irretrievably in a mail box.

"I'll stall him till... next Monday. I'll say, 'Somebody'll turn in the check. Don't worry.' By the next day or Wednesday for sure," Harry reckoned, "my roommate'll be on his way back to... wherever he's from."

Again after his recollection, Harry made no reply.

Paul pushed up his glasses, for they had slipped down a bit, and resumed his perusal of the hand. There was, he knew, an uncanny secret in its palm's inscriptions; and he took on a look of urgency. He said to Harry, "Your life line... after the second break, is creased uniformly –and for an inch and a half in length! That's understood to mean many years of unperturbed living.

"Wait!" A third break in the line had leaped into Paul's sight. "Here's a nascent break!" Setting aside the magnifying glass, Paul lowered his face to this third discovery. He ran the pencil down to it. "Mr. Clark, the length between the second and third breaks... is, I estimate, thirty years."

"Let me see," said Stella.

"But this must mean the third break is for something in the *near future*," a stupendous realization that made the epidermis of Paul's forearms prickle. "What –"

"In the near future?" A feeling of uncertainty from these words crept into Stella's mind.

But in Paul's mind a different thought arose. "Can palmistry be prophetic? I have to know. I have to think!"

Stella furrowed her brows, and Harry closed his hand. Marcie, her lips apart, asked, "What does that tell, Paul?"

Paul began searching Harry's face. "What's going to happen to Mr. Clark?" he asked himself, his own face rapt with the question. "Some calamity?"

"Paul?" Marcie took her boyfriend's arm.

"*Har-ry?*" Stella stretched the two syllables.

There was a movement toward their table, and their heads turned. A girl wearing a bombardier jacket and holding up a poster with a hand-printed advertisement on it paraded past, a meandering announcement for something happening on campus that caught and broke the Clark's attention and that jolted Paul's.

Triumph expanded across Paul's features. He felt as if a light-bulb had materialized inside his head and was now flashing; he had grasped the answer. He straightened his shoulders. The moment of perplexity had passed. "Nothing's going to happen *to him*! It's the other way around! He *did* something back then. Twice. And he's going –" He blurted out, "You've got what I need for my first story!"

"What do you need?" Stella asked, awed by everything that had transpired in the last three quarters of an hour.

"Mrs. Clark, there's a mystery lying in the palm of your husband's hand. Well– nothing horrendous." The palm reader –or palmologist, to contrive a new word –smiled conspiratorially to Harry. "Mr. Clark, my great Aunt Anna has a full run of the Fu-Manchu novels. They've cloth covers. Dark brown and dark blue cloth." Harry was listening. Paul began to pace his words. "Fourteen volumes, I remember. Anna's in her seventies. I think she'd sell those books. I could ask her."

Again, the talk among the table's occupants turned into a new direction.

Paul reached under the table and took Marcie's hand. With more assurance, more timbre in his voice, he said, "Mr. Clark! How would you like to help me –anonymously– to draft the plot of my first story?" Then: "You'll be the man behind the man who wrote the story?"

Harry rubbed his chin. He restrained himself for a moment and was about to utter his willingness –for how could he refuse it? –when Marcie spoke, her eyes fairly dancing in their sockets. "See, Daddy!"

The End

Edward Grosek has published four books, numerous magazine and journal articles and book reviews, and was from 1999 through 2009 the editor of the Rockford Writers' Guild's monthly newsletter "Write Away." Retired now from Northern Illinois University, he continues to read, study, write, and collect books.

Notes

Printed in the United States
By Bookmasters